Wrong-Way Ragsdale

CHARLES HAMMER

Farrar · Straus · Giroux

New York

For Lenore

This book is a presentation of Field Publications and Weekly Reader Books. Weekly Reader Books offers book clubs for children from preschool through high school. For further information write to: **Weekly Reader Books**, 4343 Equity Drive, Columbus, Ohio 43228.

Edited for Weekly Reader and published by arrangement with Farrar, Straus & Giroux. Weekly Reader is a federally registered trademark of Field Publications.

*Special thanks to my editor, Margaret Ferguson, who
helped me make this book*

1

ALL MY DAD ever does that he likes to do is stand out beside our fence and watch the planes take off. Our farmhouse sits off to one side of this little grass airstrip. The planes come right past us.

Sometimes an old Ercoupe with a silver fuselage and twin tails like a B-25 bomber comes down that runway. If it isn't the Ercoupe, it might be a Cessna 150 or a Stinson 108. The plane buzzes along, going faster and faster, so the pilot has to hold it on the ground. Then the pilot eases back a little, and up she goes, bouncing on the wind.

My dad just stands there looking ordinary till the plane goes up. Then he smiles and follows it with his eyes. He watches it climb into the clouds, or slowly, slowly turn into a speck against the blue sky, and the whole time he's smiling. That's about all he does that he smiles about. A boy he grew up with got to be a pilot, but my dad never did.

My dad got hitched early to the plow, that's what he says. He's worked detasseling corn and caddying for golfers and pushing bread pans into a bakery oven. He worked awhile as a hot-tar roofer. Daytimes now he de-livers soda pop to supermarkets in Kansas City, then he works nights cleaning up an office in Bonner Springs. He isn't in the union, so he gets paid lousy.

I went with him one night to clean the office. It wasn't

hard work. It was just steady, sweeping and mopping and emptying glass ashtrays. But it wore me out, and I hadn't been horsing Pepsi cases around all day. My dad has worked his butt off ever since he got married in high school.

Once I found a box of wedding pictures way deep in my mom's cedar chest. Mom is fat now. Then she looked real slim and pretty. There were two pictures of Daddy dancing with her. He had a gleam in his eye and he was smiling like he smiles when the planes go up. He was really handsome and his face was smooth. He was sixteen and a half then, and I'm already thirteen. It really gets me, thinking what it would be like to be married three years from now.

Way at the bottom of the picture box was a bill from Renshaw Photographic Studios in Springfield, Missouri. I thought that was pretty good, them sending clear to Springfield for a photographer, because they grew up in a little hick town southeast of there. The bill said my mother's father owed $90 for pictures taken on the wedding day. The date of the wedding was right there on the bill.

See, I was the first kid and the first boy. I wasn't premature, either. I weighed ten pounds three ounces. After that, they got me four sisters and a brother, bangety-bang-bang, so we got a houseful out here.

I was the first, so I'm the one that hitched my dad to the plow—Mom, too, because she grows a big garden and cans about three hundred quarts of stuff every summer and cleans house and washes all day. She just seems to like the work better than my dad does.

The only reason I'm telling you all this is because of something stupid I did. First I was going to say it was crazy, like some man on TV is a wild and crazy guy.

But it wasn't cute crazy, it was dumb crazy. More happened than you're going to believe, but I don't care. I'm gonna tell it anyway.

It started one day when my dad came in early from the Pepsi run, looking halfway happy. He went out of the house for a long time, then he finally came back with greasy black hands. I was sitting in our kitchen at the enamel tabletop eating a bowl of raisin bran for a snack, and Mom was standing at the counter with her glasses on, reading a magazine. Dad raised up his greasy black hands and started for her like the Frankenstein Monster.

"Ah!" she yelled. "Ah! Get away from me, you nasty thing!"

She started slapping at his wrists and pushing him away. Daddy is wiry and tough, but my mom is bigger than him. She is not only fat but also tall and strong. She could stick him headfirst in the wastebasket if she tried.

She didn't try. She just backed up against the wall, breathing fast and smiling. He grinned and went to the sink to wash his hands.

My dad and mom fight a lot. He hardly ever teases her funny like that. After a minute he got a beer from the refrigerator and popped the lid and sat across the table from me. He's only thirty years old, but he looks older from working out in the weather. He reached up with his hand and started pinching the scar on his left ear where about half the ear is missing. Then he lifted his beer can with his other hand and jiggled it.

"Want a sip?" he said to me. He had that funny look in his eyes, like in the wedding pictures.

"If I did, you wouldn't give it to me."

I went on eating my raisin bran. My dad is the one who's usually gloomy, he's gloomier than I am, but he said: "Hey, Mr. Sobersides, hey, Mr. Philosopher, what philosophy you been reading lately?"

All I ever read is my dad's old airplane books and hero adventure books. He's got the *Journals of Lewis and Clark* and stuff about Jimmy Doolittle and Eddie Rickenbacker and Captain Bligh and nearly everybody else. When I read it, though, he calls it philosophy.

"It's too hard for you to understand," I told him.

"Oh," he said, and his eyebrows arched up. "Well, see, all them *Joo*-ly days I was hot-tar roofing, my brain got fried in the sun like your mama's over-easy eggs. Otherwise, I would be smart as you."

He only had one drink of beer, but he was happier than most people get when they're drunk. I liked him that way.

He held out the beer can and said: "Have a sip."

I grabbed his hand and tilted the can over to take a big gulp. Then I stuck out my tongue and said, "Blaaaaaa!"

Daddy said: "You want to see something?"

"See what?"

He nodded at my bowl. "Finish your cereal. I could use a little help."

2

OUR FARMHOUSE SITS all to itself beside this air-strip. The runway is where the cropland used to be. The guy who owns the airstrip, Mr. Enright, lives in a new house like a mansion on the far side of the field.

He has a Piper Twin Comanche and four cars and about everything else you can think of. Mr. Enright never does a lick of work, but he's rich anyhow. He's like some rich king from old times, who gets everything he wants. He goes out and belts himself into his trusty craft and flies off wherever he wants to go.

My folks don't even own the house we live in, they just rent the house and one acre. We're west of De Soto, Kansas, which is west of Kansas City. There are elm and hackberry and persimmon trees along the creeks around here, and some apple orchards on the hills. Mostly it's rolling land covered with prairie grass.

After I finished the cereal, me and Daddy walked down across the garden. He opened the gate in the woven wire fence, and we went through. Then my sister Essie started squawking out an upstairs window.

"I want to go, too! I can't find my purse! You wait! If Emmett gets to go, I get to go!"

Daddy didn't fasten the gate. He stood there waiting for Essie. I didn't want to wait. I like my other sisters all right, I like Missy and Evelyn and Ethel, but I don't like Essie. She's eight years old and still sleeps with a teddy bear. She's all the time losing her things and blaming me for it. Essie eats like a pig, she even eats stuff she's allergic to, then swells up and can't breathe. Daddy has to give her a shot so she can breathe. She's a real sow pig, Essie is.

Our old black-and-tan hound, Willi, walked down from the house to go with me and Daddy. Then he got tired of waiting and walked back. After about ten years, Essie came tearing out the door and down across the garden. Her old plastic shoulder-strap purse that she got from Mama was banging against her side.

"I had to find my purse," she yelled. "Wait up! You wait!"

When she finally caught up, Dad closed the gate, and we headed up toward the cluster of airplanes and hangars. Essie went ahead of me, panting and saying, "Oh, boy . . . Oh, boy. . ." She was sweating all over. Little girls are sugar and spice, that's what I heard. An old tennis shoe is what Essie smells like when you're walking behind her. My dad kicked at the runway grass with his high-topped shoe.

"It needs cutting," he said.

"You don't need to cut that," I told him. "Old Enright doesn't pay you anything for it."

"I like to cut it," my dad said.

"Why do you do all this stuff for him? He doesn't do you any favors."

Daddy smiled as we walked, but he didn't answer. He makes me mad, working like that for nothing. Mama says he wants to be like Jimmy Doolittle, who was a great hero and flew to Tokyo when nobody else could. My dad figures he won't ever be like that. Mama tells him the guy who is good to his kids, the guy who works every day and comes home every night, that's the real hero.

Daddy doesn't believe it, so he doesn't know what to do with himself when he isn't working. That's what Mom says. He works all week, then goes out Sunday and mows old Enright's runway, just to ride the tractor and be around the planes. There's one good thing about it, though. Sometimes he helps out a certified airframe and engine mechanic. That guy's been teaching my dad how to do repairs. But Daddy is dumb to work free for old Enright. My folks pay for everything they get. Seems like Mr. Enright doesn't have to pay for anything.

Going along that line of hangars, I saw airplanes in every one, and a few planes sitting between, with their wings tied down to steel hooks in the ground. The planes were mostly rich, but the hangars were poor. The orange windsock was blown out in the toe. It's a junky little airstrip. My dad says it's just a play toy for Mr. Enright. We walked past the one new hangar where Tom Weldon has his parachute school. Tom owns the whole school and does everything himself. I looked in the open door to see him, because he's a nice guy even if he is rich, and I like talking with him. He wasn't there, but Mr. Enright's flock of guinea hens were inside, scratching under the table where Tom folds parachutes. Daddy shooed them out and pulled the door shut. Pilots don't want birds in a hangar. They'll ruin the paint on your plane and do worse than that.

Mr. Enright uses the guineas for security guards. They roost in a tree, or in this one hangar that has sides so rotted out that the guineas can crawl under. Then they set up a loud cackle if a stranger comes near the planes. That way Mr. Enright doesn't have to pay for a guard. Summertimes once in a while he'll even cook up a guinea on his barbecue grill and eat it.

We went on up the taxiway till Daddy stopped at Hangar 9, the one where the guineas roost. It's bigger than a double garage, and made of tin so rusty you can poke your finger through. We had lived by that airstrip since I was five years old, and I'd never seen the inside of it. It was like a ghost hangar to me, like it was haunted.

My dad said: "You reckon we could get inside?"

"It's locked tight," I said.

But when I took hold of the padlock, the brass part turned in my hand. I saw shiny metal on the loop where somebody had cut it with a hacksaw.

"Well, I be durned," my dad said, smiling. "Let's see what's inside."

He put the lock in his pocket and pushed with his shoulder to slide the left-hand door open.

"There's an airplane!" Essie yelled. I could see one wing of it myself. Dad came back and pushed the other door. Essie jumped in to help him. "Oh boy," she said, "there's a plane!"

They got the other door open. It was bright sunny outside and dark inside, but I could see this crappy little high-wing plane. There was about an inch of white guinea-do all over a tarp that covered the wings. Daddy walked up to the plane and stood with his hands on his hips.

"It's a Taylorcraft BC 12-D," he said. "They built it in 1947. That plane is ten years older than I am."

Both tires were flat, with the rubber pooched out to the sides on the dirt floor. There was a hole twice the size of my head in the fuselage fabric by the tail. Dust was thick all over, except around the engine cowling. The cowling was propped open, and Daddy's toolbox was sitting on a sawhorse beside it.

"I want to go in the airplane," Essie said.

"Sure, honey."

Daddy brushed the mouse turds off the seat and set

Essie up there. At first she looked plenty happy in the plane. I guess it wasn't any dirtier than her corner of the girls' second-floor bedroom. She looked out the windshield awhile, then she turned around and knelt on the seat to look back into the fuselage.

"Yaaaaaaaa!" she screamed. "Yaaaaaaaa! Something's back there! He's looking at me!"

Right then, that something bailed out of the hole in the side, like one of Tom Weldon's skydivers bails out. It went scrabbling under the tin wall of the hangar. I ran outside to see what it was. Here was this fat raccoon, with a tail about the size of George Brett's baseball bat, humping away down a little gully behind the hangars, heading for the persimmon trees.

By the time I got back inside, Essie had quieted down. She climbed out and stood there with her mouth open, looking up at the plane. She'd seen a lot of airplanes, but she knew this one was different.

"Tom Weldon talked to an old pilot he knows," Daddy told us. "Tom says this Taylorcraft was here before Mr. Enright even bought the airstrip. Some old man flew it in here Christmas Eve 1967 and just left it. That man had bought it new, with the auxiliary gas tanks. He flew just about everywhere in this plane. He flew to Alaska and Newfoundland and down to the Yucatan in Mexico. But he flew it in here that Christmas Eve and then went home to die. His heirs never did come get it."

The old man parked that airplane way before I was even born. I never saw a worse piece of junk. It looked like a ghost plane, all covered with spiderwebs and dust. It looked more like Halloween than Christmas. I'm surprised the old man didn't just die in the pilot's seat and wait for us to find him. I figured the only thing you'd ever see flying that wreck would be a skeleton.

I said: "What you want to bet, the guinea-do has rotted right through the tarp and eaten up the fabric on the wings?"

"That's what Mr. Enright thought," Dad said. "But the old man bought a good tarp. Underneath, the fabric's in fine shape."

After that, I had just one question, and I knew before I asked it what the answer would be.

"Who owns this Taylorcraft now?"

"Well," Dad answered, "it's on his place, so Mr. Enright owns it. Only he said he would give it to us. It's our airplane now."

"It's ours! It's ours!" Essie squalled. She's got a voice like razor blades scraping glass, but Daddy looked real happy.

"Mr. Enright gave it to us," Daddy said again. "Now, isn't that a pretty good favor?"

"Oh, yeah," I told him, "that's just the kind of favor Mr. Enright would do."

3

FIRST THING, DADDY tied a yellow plastic rope from the tail wheel and dropped a loop of it over a post at the back of the hangar. It was a heavy rope and a stout post. He didn't want that plane to move.

The Taylorcraft had a magneto switch, like the ignition switch in a car, but it was broken. So Daddy had spliced the wires together up front under the cowling. He had me sit in the pilot seat to work the throttle, which was a big orange ball on a steel rod that came out from the control panel. You pushed it in to give the engine more gas, only it kept sticking.

My dad wasn't trying to fly the plane, any more than you'd try to ride a dead horse you found in the pasture. He just wanted to see if the engine would work. I pounded and pounded at the throttle to make it go in. Finally it did. Dad stood in front of the plane and whirled the propeller. Nothing happened. He whirled some more. His face would rise above the engine cowling, his forehead all white where his Royals cap had shaded it from the sun. He grabbed the prop and spun again.

Couple of times he stopped and took a screwdriver to the engine. It wasn't getting gas, so he filled the auxiliary tanks in the wings to put more pressure on the line. The next time he whirled, I smelled the gas real strong.

"Now I flooded the dang carburetor," Daddy said. "Close the throttle all the way."

I yanked and yanked to get the knob out and close it down. On the next spin the engine popped, and smoke belched from the exhaust. He spun it again, and the engine started popping and coughing and spouting more smoke. Daddy ran around to my side and reached in to pound the throttle in again. It wouldn't budge. He went quick back to the engine and reached in under the cowling with a screwdriver.

"I can give it gas at the carburetor," he said.

I could see he had learned a lot from that certified mechanic guy. Pretty soon the engine ran real smooth. The propeller speeded up and kind of whizzed through the air. The plane moved a couple inches forward till the rope stopped it.

Essie came around and crawled up through the right-hand door. She said: "I'm gonna go, too. If you're gonna go, I'm gonna go."

"You already had your turn," I told her.

She crawled in and sat on the dirty seat with her big purse in her lap, like she was our mom out for a drive in the station wagon. That's one good thing my family has, a 1977 Ford station wagon with extra seats in the back to haul eight people. It's a neat car.

The Taylorcraft propeller blew wind past me and Essie like a tornado. It picked up guinea feathers from the back of the hangar and blew them forward over the plane. Then they sucked down and back through the propeller and blew around again. That plane had two sets of controls, one for me and one for idiot Essie. I pulled the yoke back and peeked around to see the elevator rise up on the tail. A kid I know at school, Billy Teegarten, his dad flies a real clean Cessna Cardinal off this airstrip. Two times they gave me a ride in that plane, and they laughed the first time, when I called the yoke a steering wheel. Mr. Teegarten let me hold the yoke anyway and sort of fly that Cardinal.

"Wings level," Mr. Teegarten told me. "Nose on the horizon. Keep your airspeed up."

Sitting there with Essie, just for devilment I tipped the yoke to one side and saw the ailerons move on the wings. That would put us in a steep bank to the left. Then I hit the left rudder pedal to turn even sharper and pushed the yoke forward to change the elevator. Back on the tail, the rudder and elevator worked. We went steep left and down. We peeled off like a Dauntless Dive Bomber chasing the enemy carriers at the Battle of Midway. I was breathing hard before I pulled out of the death dive and straightened up. Wings level, nose on the horizon, keep your airspeed up.

Those guinea feathers blew out in the sun ahead of us and lighted up, then got sucked back into the shade. That old wreck wasn't going to fly, it wasn't even going to roll on those flat tires. But I felt like I was flying through a cloud of guinea feathers. Daddy stood in front, grinning at us.

Then Mr. Enright came up behind my dad, carrying a whisky glass about the size of a Mason jar. He wears jeans a lot, just like my dad wears jeans, but you can see how different Mr. Enright's are. They're Alexander Julian jeans or sometimes other kinds so soft and rich and expensive nobody's ever heard of them.

Maybe you don't think the brand of jeans is all that much, but I got in a fight over it once. About the time Billy Teegarten had been at De Soto Junior High School long enough to feel cocky, he booted me in the butt with his toe and called me the K mart Kid. I went right at him. That's what I figured out, when they pick on you, go at 'em. Whether you win or lose, they'll be slower to start it next time. Billy bloodied my nose, he won the fight, but afterwards we got to be pretty good friends.

Anyway, Mr. Enright walked up in his Alexander Julian jeans and laid a hand on Daddy's shoulder. My dad kind of wilted and started ducking his head, like Mr. Enright was his boss or something, while they yelled back and forth over the engine noise. I felt bad when I saw it.

Then Mr. Enright pushed the glass of booze up to my dad's mouth and made him take a sip. Myself, before I would drink after Mr. Enright, I would rather drink after our hound, Willi, whose breath smells like glue. Mr. Enright's face was red, he was halfway staggering as usual. He's in investments, that's what my dad says. I guess when you're in investments, you can be drunk all the time and nobody fires you off your job.

I wanted to cut the engine and hear what they were saying, but Daddy had turned the gas on at the carburetor. When he saw me pointing at the cowling, he reached in with his screwdriver and killed the engine. Suddenly that hangar was quiet, I never heard anything so quiet. But Mr. Enright kept on yelling: "*Norton, I sure never thought you'd get that old thing started.*" He looked around like he was waking up. "Whooo-eeee!" he said, his voice sounding normal again. "If you leave an old engine sitting for years, it'll seize up and rust on you. But that one sounds better than my Comanche."

"I cleaned it out and overhauled the carburetor," my dad said. "That engine's old, Mr. Enright, but before the old man died he must've had it remanufactured and packed for storage. It's perfect. It's a perfect old Taylorcraft engine."

My dad calls him Mister all the time, but to him my dad is always just Norton. Old Enright stumbled around and came up to the cabin door beside me. He smelled somewhere between Dentyne gum and an empty Jack Daniel's bottle I found one day beside the road.

He ruffled my hair and said: "Howya doing, sonny?"

To him, us Ragsdale kids are just sort of a flock like his flock of guineas. He's known me since I was five years old, I babysit his grandsons, and he still doesn't know my name. He didn't say one word to Essie. He probably figured there are so many girls in our family you don't have to talk to them. He went up and looked under the engine cowling, breathing kind of deep and rocking from side to side.

"Whoooo-eeeeeeee! Well, I want David to see this. David's gonna think it's really something. I never thought to hear the engine run like *that*. I didn't think you'd even get it started."

David is old Enright's son-in-law. David's kids are the ones I babysit. David's not so bad, but he gets drunk, too, and he isn't even in investments.

Guinea fluff was still floating down. I smelled it scorching on the hot cylinder heads. Enright wrinkled his nose and started brushing fluff off his shirtsleeves and looking up with blood-veined eyes, real confused. He wondered whether it was a real snowstorm or something from the whisky in his head.

Then he fished a soppy feather out of his glass and said: "Aha! Aha!" So he wasn't going crazy, after all.

Old Enright walked out from under the fluff and turned to look back at the plane. He looked at the cowling where the engine was.

"Whoooo-eeeeeee!" he said again.

Then he turned and walked away toward his mansion on the other side of the airstrip. Just from the way he looked at the engine, I knew how it would turn out, but my dad didn't.

4

DADDY KEPT WORKING every weekend on the airplane, with me helping sometimes. He found a wrecked Taylorcraft at the little Basehor airport and bought the tires and wheels from it, so the tires on our plane weren't flat anymore. He bought new spark plugs and other stuff and really tuned the engine fine. It sounded better than anything on the airstrip. The raccoon got so used to Daddy that he kept right on sleeping in his nest in the tail.

Most Sundays, Mom would go up there and talk to Daddy while he worked. Once she fried up a bunch of chicken backs and chicken wings, and we had us a picnic where the hangar shaded the ground. We sat around a blanket spread on the grass, and all the kids were there. My dad had a friend named Emmett. He was the one who got to be a pilot. That's how I got my name. Then Mom followed the E for a while to name Evelyn and Ethel and Essie. She finally decided that E business was too country, so she named the last kids Robert and Missy.

Anyhow, we were all there eating fried chicken. Essie pulled her usual dirty trick. She took the biggest chicken back and ate off the crisp skin, which is the best part. She put the piece back on the plate for some dumb cluck to finish. Then she got a new piece and ate the skin off that one, too. Essie is a true sow pig.

One day Mama found some biscuits under Essie's pillow and a wad of cheese stuffed in the toe of an old shoe in the closet. Another time it was Fig Newtons in Essie's footlocker. Ann Landers says kids who hide food are insecure, that's what Mama told Daddy. Mama said the two of them had to quit fighting, because it made Essie insecure. Myself, I don't think Essie is insecure. She's just a pig.

"Quit hogging the chicken skin," I told her. "You're gonna turn red from the allergy and swell up so you can't breathe."

She looked mean at me and blew her cheeks up with air. I blew mine up right back at her. About then, Robert reached over and grabbed a chicken back that Ethel already had her fingers on.

Ethel said: "Let go, you little skunk."

"No!" Robert yelled.

He's little, all right, but he's tough. Robert and Ethel get along about like me and Essie. Mom didn't bawl them out. She just reached in between and took that piece of chicken for herself. Then she turned toward the hangar and changed the subject.

"Why, look there, Norton. You patched the hole in the tail. How will the coon get in and out?"

Daddy was gnawing a chicken back that my sow sister had skinned. He said: "I leave the cabin door open. No sense running him out. That coon might die of old age before we ever get this plane to fly."

What he said wasn't funny, but we all smiled, anyway. My dad sat on the grass looking at the airplane, and we were all smiling at him. It made me think we were like a happy family on TV, like on *Little House on the Prairie*. That's about the first time I remember thinking I was in a happy family.

We had a good time like that for a whole month,

hanging around the Taylorcraft while my dad worked on
it. I helped. I cleaned the inside and dusted the old
maps we found behind the seat. One day he told me to
look at the front of the propeller and tell him the color.
I said silver. Then he had me crawl in the cabin.

"Now what color is the prop?"

"On this side it's black."

"Why is that?"

It smelled old in the cabin, like our basement. I sat
there a minute.

"I don't know," I told him. "Why's it silver in front
and black behind?"

"So the sun won't reflect in the pilot's eyes. See, who-
ever designed this propeller, he thought it out. People
going high in the air, he didn't want 'em killed because
he built it stupid." Dad reached in and slid his hand
along the top of the control panel, like he was petting
it. "That guy built it right."

He put one finger on a dial that said CLIMB and told
how, if you get lost in a cloud, it shows whether you're
going up or down. He told me about RPM and CARBU-
RETOR HEAT and PRIMER and ALTIMETER. While he
talked, I looked on past the black prop and out of the
hangar. There wasn't any sun that day to blind a pilot.
Gray rain drizzled down on the green runway.

A plane was coming through it from the north, slanting across in front of the hangar. It flared out and
touched down smooth on the grass. It was Tom Weldon's blue Cessna 180, but my dad didn't look. He
pointed to a handle thing inside the Taylorcraft above
the right door, like the handle of a faucet. The sign
above it said: FILL MAIN TANK IN LEVEL FLIGHT ONLY.
There was another handle like it over the left door.

"When you fly so far you run out of gas in the main
tank," my dad said, "that's how you get the auxiliary gas

18

down to the engine. You can fly six hours, you can fly five hundred miles on all three tanks."

Looking around the inside of the cabin, I started to like the people who built the Taylorcraft. Everything in there was old and crummy, but it was also tiny and neat and fixed to keep the pilot safe.

Daddy jumped all of a sudden at a big boom of thunder. I jumped, too. The tin roof of the hangar started singing loud, and the rain came down. It really poured. Wind blew a plywood box—bang—against the side of our hangar.

The storm boomed and thundered so loud we didn't hear Tom's plane till he whirled it around in front of the hangar and cut the engine. He jumped out and ran like a fool for the door, carrying a parachute. Rainwater ran from his hair and dripped off his nose. He was panting in a way that sounded like laughing.

He looked at my dad and yelled: "I saw that one coming, Norton. Figured I'd rather be on the ground than up there in it. Can I hang out here for five minutes?"

"You bet, Tom."

Tom smiled at me and said, "Howya doing, Emmett?"

I told him pretty good. He stood there looking at the Taylorcraft. He was wearing neat coveralls made out of shiny blue stuff. Tom held the parachute by a strap that went over his shoulder so it hung on his back like a knapsack. He kept rocking on his toes, so that parachute bounced off his back and swung out and bounced again. He had on his fancy gold watch that can time just about anything. It'll time the seconds you fall and then ring like an alarm clock to remind you to open the chute before you hit the ground—that's what Tom told me. Tom is rich, he owns the 180 and another Cessna besides, but he works hard to stay rich. He waved the hand with the watch up at the Taylorcraft.

"Norton, if you're gonna fly that, why don't you first come and learn to jump."

My dad stuck his hands in the back pockets of his jeans and looked at the ground. "If I ever get the plane ready, then I got to take flying lessons and buy a pilot's license. I don't know when I'll have money for parachute lessons."

"Talk to me anyhow when you get to the right place," Tom said. "You already helped me fold enough parachutes. I'll give you a rate."

"Thanks. Maybe I'll get the chance."

The storm boomed again, but the rain was less. Tom and Daddy walked over to the door. Tom stuck his hand out in the rain and looked at the sky, but my dad was watching him. Tom kept rocking on his toes, and the parachute kept bouncing against his blue coveralls. He's not as handsome as my dad; he's older, too, but his skin is smooth and young. He looked like Douglas Bader or maybe Richard Hillary at Hornchurch airdrome in England, like he was ready to climb in his Spitfire and fly through the clouds to shoot down a Heinkel bomber or dogfight an ME-109.

My dad said: "I had one friend from high school who got to be a pilot. He was a lot like you."

"What?" Tom asked. "Was he crazy—working twelve hours a day trying to run a business?"

"Naw," my dad said. "He was just kind of like you."

Tom looked at my dad like he didn't know what to say. Daddy pulled his hands out of his pockets and shrugged and turned away smiling.

Tom smiled, too, and said: "Gotta go." He walked out through the drizzle to his 180. He crawled in and yelled, "Remember what I said."

Then, before you could say Jimmy Doolittle, Tom

started his engine and revved it to wheel the Cessna and take off through the rain.

It was fun, all the people we saw and all the work we did on the Taylorcraft. Just when it was getting good, I found a summer job sacking groceries at the Fleming Brothers Super in De Soto. Couple of years ago, I used to shoplift from them. Sometimes on winter days before the school bus came, they let us kids stand in there to keep warm, so I stole their candy bars and gum.

I thought I was smart, being so sneaky. Right then, I was reading about somebody else sneaky, an old-time guy named Douglas Corrigan, who was a mechanic on Charles Lindbergh's plane before Lindbergh flew across the Atlantic Ocean.

Later on, Corrigan wanted to fly across the Atlantic, too. He had such a lousy plane the government wouldn't let him. He filled it up with gas and told 'em he would fly to California. First thing you know, he landed in Ireland and said he must've gone the wrong way. He never did anything as wrong as I did, but they called him Wrong-Way Corrigan, because he was sneaky and daring. I was sneaky like Corrigan, I thought I was daring, and I wanted to be like him. So I started thinking I was Wrong-Way Ragsdale.

Anyhow, I used to steal from Fleming Brothers and still they were always nice to me. Now, I got to work there when I was really too young. They paid me the minimum wage, too, which didn't seem minimum to me. It was $3.35 an hour. That's way better than the buck an hour David pays for babysitting. But it made me feel weird, because I knew my dad got paid only $4 an hour for his night janitor job.

See, except for your family and friends, nobody gives a hoot about you. You can be thirty years old and have six children and still get paid about the same as a kid. Finding that out scared me a little. I saw how my dad really was hitched to the plow and wondered if I would be hitched, too. I started thinking, at least Daddy has an airplane, at least he can work on it and maybe someday learn to fly it. That's what I was hoping, till everything busted loose.

5

IT STARTED ON a Sunday afternoon. Mom gave me dinner before the others, so I could get out to weed the garden. It was warm summer, with orange tomatoes already on the vines. I chopped at the weeds, dreading having to call her out to see how well I'd done the job. She would make me rake up all the weeds, and underneath she'd find about a million weeds I'd missed. Then she would make me do it over. When I was little, I bawled if she made me do it over, but I quit that long ago.

I was still cutting weeds when I heard the Taylorcraft engine start. It sputtered a couple of times, then the sound came smooth down to me across the green runway. It's only got 65 horsepower, it's the smallest engine on the field, so it sounds different. Daddy came out on the back porch, wiping his mouth on a paper napkin and looking up toward the hangars. Mom was right behind him.

"Norton, why don't you finish your dinner."

"I better see what's going on."

"I'll go with you," I told him.

Essie popped out from behind Mama with jelly bread in her hand. "I'm gonna go, too. If Emmett's gonna go, I'm gonna go."

Then Robert squeezed in between and started down, taking the steps one at a time. He was holding the rail and everything, but Mom said: "Come back here, Robert." She caught him under the arms and lifted. He squalled like fury. "I wanna go! I wanna go!"

"You get back in there and eat your dinner."

Mom held him out, kicking and squirming like a mad rat, till she set him back inside. That took care of Robert, but I figured now the rest of the pack would want to come—Evelyn and Ethel and Missy. Maybe they were still hungry, though, because they didn't. 'Course there wasn't any stopping Essie. She trailed us up the runway with that scabby handbag flapping on her hip and jelly bread in her hand—old oink-oink Essie. Around our house, biscuits kept disappearing, and the whole-wheat Fig Newtons had also. That week Mama lost a whole box of Hershey's Big Block candy bars, which she bought for family treats. Mama thought she just misplaced it, the candy will turn up, she said. But so far it hadn't.

As long as we were going up the runway, our hound, Willi, decided he might as well go, too. We scared up grasshoppers as we walked, and the guineas started following to gobble them up. If everybody else in the whole world was going, why shouldn't the guineas go, too?

Hangar 9 faces the other way from our house. We curved out to the east to see what was happening. First I saw the Porsche sports car that belongs to David, Mr. Enright's son-in-law, parked to one side. Then I saw the plane in the hangar, with David walking around on the grass in front, carrying a whisky glass. He was pointing at the plane with his free hand and yelling over the engine noise to Enright, who was standing off to one side. By that time, they had slowed the engine down to idle. I looked at them and started getting mad.

"What's old Enright doing with your airplane?" I asked my dad.

"All he did is start the engine."

"He didn't ask you first. That makes me mad."

"Now just cool off, Emmett. He's our neighbor. He gave us that plane."

Up ahead, David put his whisky down on the grass and waved both arms, talking to Mr. Enright real excited.

David saw us and walked out to meet my dad. "It's running great," he said. "I never heard one sound so good."

"It does run good," Daddy said.

By then, Willi had started sniffing after rabbits in tall grass out to the left side of the taxiway. A pile of angle iron and beat-up car fenders kept the mower from cutting there. Not that my dad ever gets to go hunting, but Willi is supposed to be a foxhound. He's not supposed to chase rabbits.

My dad looked at him out there and yelled: "Hyaaaaaaa, Willi! You quit that!"

Willi looked real guilty and slunk over to where Essie was feeding the guineas. She chunked off pieces of her jelly bread, and the guineas made that crazy beep-beep sound like their adenoids were bad.

David walked around real happy in his expensive loafers. They were lizard-skin loafers, that's what David told me one time when I asked him.

"This airframe is pretty bad," he was saying, "but I found a dandy Taylorcraft airframe in a hangar over at Basehor. The fabric's been redone on that one. Just the engine is bad, that's the only thing wrong with it."

Old Enright came walking up to us with his whisky glass, looking half funny and half worried about something. He waved his other hand up at the propeller,

25

which was spinning as the engine idled, and said: "Norton, I'll pay you for them new spark plugs and carburetor parts. Maybe I could give you a little for your time, too."

Right then, my face started burning. I started getting hot all over. My head began to ache. Daddy got a little pale in the face. He said: "That's my Taylorcraft, Mr. Enright. You gave that airplane to me."

"You did!" I screamed at him. "You gave it to him!" Enright didn't even look at me. He said, "Norton, Norton. . ." and put his arm around my dad's shoulders. "Come around where we can talk, Norton. Sonny, you stay here."

"The heck I will!" I said.

"Emmett, stay here," my dad said.

So I had to stay. This time Essie didn't try to tag along with Daddy. She just looked surprised at all the yelling. David followed Daddy and Mr. Enright way out to one side of the hangar, far enough so they thought I couldn't hear. I could hear, though, because I sneaked up inside the hangar and looked out through a hole in the tin siding. I saw my dad stand with his back straight like a broomstick and argue with Mr. Enright. Say that for my dad, he did some yelling, and Enright started yelling back.

"I gave you the airplane, I didn't give you the engine! Now they tell me over at Basehor that a remanufactured engine is worth two thousand dollars. I don't give away money like that."

"David can buy any kind of plane," my dad said. "What does he want with an old Taylorcraft?"

That puzzled Enright for a minute. He shook his ice cubes in the glass till whisky splashed his hand. "I don't know," he said. "He thinks it's cute. He wants it, and he's going to get it."

26

That's when the broomstick started coming out of my dad's back. He's a little guy anyway, and he seemed to get littler. Watching it, I thought I would choke. I thought I would never breathe again.

David didn't even have to be in the argument. He just stood off to the side by his Porsche and watched. David didn't have to work for anything. He didn't even have to argue for it. He always won everything and got everything he wanted. When you're a kid and somebody picks on you, you can go right at 'em. But when you're a grownup like my dad, you can't.

I was so hot in my head I couldn't hear for a minute. Then I started hearing the engine again. I turned around and saw the Taylorcraft with its propeller still going around in idle. That airplane was rotten and filthy and had guinea crap all over, but it was the only plane my dad was ever going to own. Without the engine, it was nothing.

I never *decided* to do anything, like they tried to say later. I never decided. I just started doing it.

6

THE YELLOW ROPE tied to the tail wheel was still looped over the post at the back of the hangar. I lifted it off and dropped it on the ground. Out front of the hangar, Willi and Essie were standing side by side, looking in at me.

"Emmett, what are you doing?" Essie yelled. "You better not!"

I held the wing strut and started to crawl into the pilot's seat. My dad's old wooden toolbox was on it. I pushed the box over to the other side and got in. The throttle was stuck on idle. I pounded the orange ball till the throttle broke free and went all the way in. The engine buzzed up quick, and the plane started shaking. Guinea feathers fogged up all around. The right-hand door popped open, and Essie reached her hand up for a hold. She was standing on the steel step of the plane.

"Get out!" I pushed her back and leaned over far enough to see the ground on that side slowly moving under the wheels. "You stay out!"

"If you get to go, I get to go!"

She jumped up again and grabbed the seat, then started pulling her dumb shoulder-strap purse in through the door. She took hold like a boa constrictor with her jelly-bread fingers. I couldn't bust her loose.

"Get out, you crazy fool!"

But she wouldn't get out. We rolled out of the hangar

into bright sunlight. I turned to the front as we rocked over the rough ground toward the flock of guineas. They stopped eating the bread scraps and started walking away, looking at me real uneasy over their shoulders. It was hard to see them, because the Taylorcraft is a tail-dragger. You see lots of sky through the windshield and not much ground. Through the side window I caught a glimpse of Willi running along with us, baying his head off.

"Whooo! Wharooooop!"

There was so much noise and shaking and scary stuff going on I couldn't think. Essie turned around and sat down on the toolbox.

"Get out, Essie! Get out!"

"Anything you get to do," she said, "I get to do it, too."

She is the worst sister in the world. I pity anybody else who has a sister like her. Next time I looked, it wasn't just guineas on the taxiway ahead of us, it was also my dad and David and old Enright. They waved, and their mouths opened and closed. It was like watching TV with the sound turned off, because I couldn't hear much over the plane's engine except for Willi. He was loud. Then, inside the plane, I heard Essie yell: "You're gonna hit Daddy!"

I pulled at the throttle to stop us. It wouldn't pull. I yanked at it, but it wouldn't come out. Daddy was a little to the left, waving his arms and walking toward us. The plane turned to the right. They tried to say after wards that I turned it, but I didn't. Maybe the Taylor-craft just didn't like David and Mr. Enright, because it went right at them. Daddy came running in from the side and then fell. He fell down hard over a piece of angle iron in that pile beside the taxiway.

Mr. Enright and David waved real wild at me. Their

eyes got big. Essie stood up from the toolbox and turned around, like she couldn't stand to see us run over the two men. But when she glanced behind us down the inside of the fuselage, she said:

"Yaaaaaa! He's looking at me! He's coming up here!" She cringed back against the windshield. Next thing I knew, the big raccoon was standing behind her seat. He grabbed the seat back with little black hands and swung his head over, looking out through his black mask. He was panting and saying, "Wuff! Wuff! Wuff!" That coon was bad scared.

"Yaaaaaaa!" Essie squalled. "Get him out! Get him out!"

I didn't know how to get him out. The plane was shaking, and chunks of guinea crap the size of a dinner plate were breaking loose and falling off the tarpaulins on the wings. I could see Willi out Essie's side window, running and jumping up to look at the coon through the glass.

David and Mr. Enright ran ahead of us down the taxiway. Why did they do that? Why didn't they get out of the way? They ran backward and waved and moved their lips, yelling cuss words I couldn't hear. All this time they had been looking real mad at me, but right about then they started looking scared, instead. That's when they stopped running backward and turned around and started running forward. The raccoon kept saying, "Wuff," and scratching at Essie's door, which is the one my dad always left open for him.

"Let him out, you idiot!" I yelled.

Essie's mouth was set like she tasted something nasty. She hissed: "You are not the boss of me!"

I hated her. I really hated her. I had to lean over in the seat to reach the door handle, and the coon bailed out. He looked happy getting out, till old Willi got after him. The coon couldn't outrun the hound. He scooted up and started dodging back and forth between David and Mr. Enright, trying to hide behind them as they ran. Willi was all white teeth and red mouth.

"Woooo! Woooo! Woooof!"

He wanted to eat that coon. They went twice around Mr. Enright. Then Enright fell over the hound, and they dropped behind us. David was still up there, though. He was running flat out. The soles of his lizard loafers just flashed as he ran. To keep from being trompled by him, the guineas started flapping their wings and running faster. One of David's loafers flipped off. He was running and limping on that stocking foot and halfway falling down. He turned to look back just as the plane caught up.

Then I remembered the rudder pedals. I tapped one pedal and turned us to the right. We went past him toward the runway and toward the guineas. The whole bunch zoomed up in the air like a covey of quail, flying straight down the runway ahead of us.

That's when the tarpaulins flew up and flapped off behind. They took the worst of the guinea crap with them, and all of a sudden the wings worked better. The plane felt lighter. The runway wasn't rough like the taxiway. It was smooth with big easy swells like the ocean. Without the roughness, we rolled faster. The persimmon trees just whizzed by.

We came up really quick on a big pole barn to the left of the runway, where the farmer used to store hay. Like a flash, I thought I would turn with the rudder pedals and run into the barn to stop us. But the Taylorcraft was full of gas that could burn us up, and I was too scared to try. I remembered the magneto switch on the control panel and flipped it, off and on, and off and on. It still didn't work. I pounded at that throttle knob and yanked back. It wouldn't come out.

The green runway turned to a blur underneath, and I saw telephone wires at the end. We would roll up one of those swells and roll down hard to the bottom and then roll up the next one. All of a sudden we weren't rolling on the tail wheel anymore. The tail rose up, so I saw less sky and more ground through the windshield. It looked lots safer till we went up the next swell on the front wheels, and I braced myself for the bump when we hit bottom. There wasn't any bump. We were floating glassy smooth about a thousand miles an hour straight toward the telephone wires.

That's when we caught up with the guineas. To get out of our way, they turned and sort of exploded every which direction, all except one of them, which tried to outfly the plane.

"Don't!" I yelled. "Don't, you crazy fool!"

He went "Splaaaaaaaat!" on the propeller. That was one guinea old Enright never got to barbecue. It was like somebody dropped that guinea in my mother's Waring blender, which she bought for $3 at a garage sale. Tiny gobs of red guinea goo flew out and stuck to the windshield and the wings and the engine cowling and everything else. We were plastered up everywhere with guinea goo and guinea crap and guinea feathers.

I was so scared I thought my eyeballs would pop out in my hands. But it was all just cotton candy to Essie. She sat up on her toolbox, looking out and grinning like she was on the Zambezi Zinger at Worlds of Fun. When we rose up over the telephone wires, she said:

"Wheeeeeeeeeeeeee!"

7

'COURSE YOU WOULDN'T be hearing this if I got killed, so you know I lived through it. That doesn't mean I didn't kill Essie with my stupid stunt. That doesn't mean I didn't crash the Taylorcraft into a house and kill a dozen other people. I could be telling this from a hospital bed somewhere, bandaged up like a mummy with everything broken for the rest of my life. I could be telling it from jail.

I found out later from Tom Weldon that it's not too hard getting an airplane up. It's not too hard flying around for a while. What's hard is getting it down with everybody still alive. Plenty of dumb clucks have been squashed bloody or burned black doing that. Maybe that's why I'm telling it at all—so you can find out what it's like without doing dumb stuff that might make all those bad things happen.

I didn't know any of this while the old Taylorcraft was staggering along with treetops and the haymows of barns zipping by about two inches under Daddy's new tires. I sat gripping the yoke like death and saying, "Wings level, nose on the horizon, keep your airspeed up. . ." I kept worrying we would find one tree a little higher than the rest of them. "Wings level, nose on the horizon. . ."

None of this bothered old Essie. She still thought she was on the Zambezi Zinger, and it was starting to get

33

boring. About the time that tall tree did show up ahead of us, she said: "Make us go higher!"

I pulled back on the yoke. Then I couldn't see green anymore over the engine cowling. I saw blue sky and felt the push on the seat of my pants.

"Zooooo-o-o-oom!" Essie yelled.

But I could feel us going slower, I could just *feel* it. The propeller started whizzing real weird. Keep your airspeed up. Keep it up! Nose on the horizon! I pushed the yoke back to the middle. It was like going over the highest hump on the Zinger, where your stomach rises up inside about even with your ears.

"Oooo-o-o-o-oo. . ." Essie groaned.

Over the cowling I could see green trees again, only they were tiny because we were high. I started remembering what Mr. Teegarten said, that in an airplane it's not speed that kills you, it's stopping in the middle of the air. You pull up too much, then the plane stalls and dives straight down. Wings level, nose on the horizon. . .It worked pretty good. I turned the yoke to the left. The plane banked and turned a little. I was surprised the Taylorcraft did what I told it to. When I straightened the yoke again, the plane leveled out and quit turning. Essie pounded her feet on the floor.

"More! Do it more!"

She was still sitting on Daddy's toolbox. I told her to put it behind the seat, figuring she would fight me about it. But she was having such a good time she did just what I said. Then she saw this tiny red speck high up near the sun.

"Let's go see the balloon," she said.

"That's just guinea goo on the windshield," I told her. But it was a balloon, which wasn't only red but was also purple and green and yellow. It was painted to look like the gumball machine at Fleming Brothers Super, only where the gum comes out, two men and a woman were hanging in a basket. They were drinking something out of wineglasses like they do at Mr. Enright's house when I babysit up there.

When we passed the balloon, the people in it pointed at the Taylorcraft and laughed. They thought the guinea crap and guinea feathers were funny. One of them reached up to a handle over his head and made fire shoot up in the balloon. We were just the riffraff, see, and they rose high above us. We flew in the shadow of the balloon. I saw sun shining through its colors. I thought what great things rich people get to do, they go floating around the sky in a balloon or fly away in their own airplanes.

Then I remembered *I* was flying a plane. I myself. For about a minute my head filled up with cotton candy, too. I saw a puffy cloud and dove right for it. It came at us sudden. Essie flinched back and yelled: "Yaaaaaaaaa!" But she was grinning when we came out the other side. I thought, Wheeeeeeee, I'm flying an airplane. We leveled out.

"More! Do it more!" Essie yelled.

But she didn't close her mouth. She sat with her mouth open, looking at the wing on my side. Halfway out on the wing, a three-cornered hunk of fabric had come loose and folded back and was flapping like mad. You could see the steel tubing inside the wing. Out near the tip, another piece was peeling slowly back. That's the first time Essie noticed where we were, and what kind of fix we were in. It scared her. It scared me, too, because the hole in the wing started pulling the plane to the left. My hands got ice-cold steadying the yoke, and I started looking around.

We were so high that trucks on the highway straight below looked like my brother Robert's toys. We were so high I bet we could see Topeka, I bet we could see Saint Joe, but that far away everything turned into haze. We were flying all alone between green ground and the blue sky that went up forever. Essie closed her mouth and said: "We're lost, Emmett. Aren't we lost?"

"We aren't either lost," I told her.

"We'll never find our way," she said, and her pouty lips quivered.

"Don't you start bawling, Essie."

"You're the bawl-baby," she hissed. "You're the one that bawls when Mama makes you cut the weeds."

I was glad she fought me back. I didn't want her to cry now.

"Look there," I said. "It's an airport. That's where we've been headed ever since we took off."

8

ALL THE TIME I was lying, because I was lost just like she said. But I did see an airport. It was a big one with paved runways for airplanes to land on and a dozen paved taxiways, so they could taxi to the hangars. Essie stared out through the windshield, real excited.

"I see it, too!" Like everything I had told her was true, and pretty soon we'd be home again.

We crept slowly closer to the airport till the control tower came in sight. I couldn't ask for permission to land, because we didn't have a radio. I didn't know how I was going to land with the engine running flat out and the throttle still stuck, but I took us down and tried. We came in over a road and telephone wires, over a fence till I was almost to the runway. Then there was a giant roar on Essie's side.

Zooming right past us was a jet fighter with its flaps curved out and its wheels reaching down, sort of leaning back and flying like an anvil flies, because it was so heavy and the wings were so small.

We were going flat out, and the jet was going as slow as it could fly, and still it passed us at about a hundred miles an hour. The pilot's white helmet turned. He gawked at our old Taylorcraft. Then—whoooooooooo-osh!—the jet plane was landing on the runway ahead of us while we were still fifty feet in the air. My eyeballs tried to pop out in my hands again, and we got caught in the tornado his plane left behind. We tossed and bounced and tipped and nearly stood on our heads. Essie screamed:

"Emmett, I'm scared!"

I just held on to the yoke. Wings level, nose on the horizon . . . We leveled off and came staggering up again. I was panting and my hands had ridges and wrinkles where I gripped the yoke. I felt sick, because I had nearly killed that fighter pilot and us, too.

We flew over more telephone wires and a house and on away from the airport. After the jet plane, I didn't want to go near any airport. That's when I saw a giant brick building that said Marion Labs on the front. It was the first thing I'd seen on the whole flight that I had seen before. So I knew where we were, but where was that?

I turned across some freeways and saw two swimming pools in the back yards of two next-door houses. One was blue and the other was gray. I knew I had seen those pools before. I started thinking about riding beside Dad in the station wagon on the way to Grandpa and Grandma's house in the Ozarks. That's when I had seen the swimming pools and the Marion Labs building. This was where we always turned off on Highway 71 to Grandpa and Grandma's house. Still, I didn't know what to do.

We kept flying in a big circle, and I kept feeling sick, which is also the way I felt after I shoplifted and stole stuff from the Fleming Brothers Super. It kind of hit me then that everybody would think I had stolen something else. It was Mr. Enright's plane, or anyhow his engine, and they would think I stole it. I was Wrong-Way Ragsdale again. I didn't see how I could go home, even if I knew which way home was.

Essie said: "You weren't really going to that airport. You don't know *where* we're going."

"Yes, I do," I told her.

"We're *lost*!" Essie wailed. "We're never gonna find our way!"

Tears came out of her eyes and snot dripped from her nose. I hated to see her cry when it was my fault. That's what happens when you feel guilty about something wrong you did. You cover it up by doing something wronger.

"We're not either lost," I told Essie. "I know right where we're headed."

"Where?"

I didn't know where, but my mouth did. It said: "We're going to Grandpa and Grandma's house."

"They died," Essie said. "We can't go there."

"It's a hideout we're going to, a hideout on a mountain not too far from their old house."

"Why do we need a hideout?"

"See, Essie, people will think we stole this plane. We better hide out for a while."

She looked at me with her ratty tan eyes and said: "I sure didn't steal any airplane."

"Well, dang it, they'll think *I* did!" I yelled. "Why the dickens did you have to come along?"

She didn't answer back. After a while I glanced over and saw one tear roll down her cheek. She wiped it away with her hand and took some shuddery breaths. Boy, she makes me mad. One time she's so mean she scratches your eyes out, next time she cries if you even say something to her.

In a minute she started breathing ordinary and said: "But what place *is* it?"

"You know that Indian arrowhead on Daddy's dresser?"

"Uh-huh."

It wasn't really an arrowhead. It was a lance point made by some Indians who hunted mastodons seven thousand years ago. That's what this expert guy said after Daddy showed him the flint point. He told us a mastodon was an old-time elephant about the size of a Ford pickup, only taller. But Essie didn't care about that.

"Well," I told her, "that's where we're going—where the Indian arrowhead came from."

"Oh," she said, and sat back, real happy. She trusted me. I felt guilty because she trusted me.

But the nose of the Taylorcraft came slowly around till I could see Highway 71 going south ahead of us, a million cars on it and bridges that crossed over, with everything getting smaller till I couldn't see any farther through the haze.

That's where I aimed us, right at the middle of the haze, while I tried to remember what my dad had told me about the cave and the mountain where the mastodon hunters lived. If we were ever going to find it, I had to remember.

9

I WASN'T WITH my dad the first time he found the lance point, but I was the second time. That was last fall down on the south Missouri farm where he grew up. I got tired of being in the house with the other kids. My dad was in the barn, so I went out there.

I had spent part of two summers on that place with Grandpa and Grandma Ragsdale, but I had never seen the barn like it was last fall. It was empty. You could see just the tire prints of the manure spreader on the dirt floor, which was all that was left of the machines. They had already sold the machines at the auction.

See, my granddad died a month before that, right in the middle of losing his farm. My grandma was already so sick she was about to die. And my dad had just finished selling it all, the machinery and house and cattle and that whole half section of land to pay off the loan.

He didn't act sad about it. He was walking back and forth real brisk on the stable floor. He found a handsaw and a little anvil and a wooden toolbox that didn't get sold in the auction. He carried stuff load by load over to the door, so it would be ready to take home with us to De Soto.

It was dark on that stable floor with the loft above it, but I could see old horse harnesses hung up on nails, bridles and surcingles and long reins for plow horses.

My granddad had told me the horses were already gone before he bought the farm.

I touched one leather bridle. It was black and stiff as strap iron. I smelled the bran and the cracked corn and the cattle that used to be there. I think I even smelled the horses that wore the harnesses long ago. Daddy finished with the tools and climbed up a ladder through a hole to the loft. I went right after him.

It was light up there. The morning sun came in the big hay door on the east side. It came through cracks in the walls and a million tiny holes between the roof shingles. It shined like laser beams on dust in the air and on the cloud from my dad's breath, because the day was cold. Maybe my dad was getting zapped with a million laser beams from *Star Wars*, because he acted like he was zapped.

He'd been walking around fast, but now he just stood in the middle of the loft floor on some scraps of hay, which was the only thing left. He stood so quiet I could hear the river running over rocks in the valley down below. It was like he suddenly remembered something—not just one thing but a lot of things at the same time.

"We used to play up here," he said. "We hauled a couple of sawhorses up from the shop. I lived on a farm and didn't have a horse, but we had a good time *playing* horse."

He walked to the east wall and climbed up a slanting brace almost to the underside of the roof shingles. Coming down, he held on with just one hand because he was carrying a box in the other.

"What's in the box?" I asked.

He sat down cross-legged where the sun came in the hay door, and he leaned back on the doorframe. It was an old Cream of Wheat box. He pulled a paperback book out and looked at the cover and stuffed it in the pocket of his jean jacket.

"What's that?" I asked him.

"None of your nosy business."

I bet it was a dirty book. I bet I got a book dirtier than that rolled up and hid in the toe of a boot in my closet. Daddy reached in the box and pulled out a little cloth sack that said Bull Durham on the side.

"That's smoking tobacco, Emmett. That's fifteen-year-old smoking tobacco."

In the box he found a pack of cigarette papers sticky on one edge. He licked one sheet and rolled a cigarette out of the Bull Durham.

"Have a smoke," he said, and gave it to me.

That surprised me. He never smokes. Mom would've killed us if she had come out and caught us smoking. But he rolled himself a cigarette and lighted his and mine with matches from the box—fifteen-year-old matches. The Bull Durham tasted like bull something else, but I smoked it. I didn't get sick, either.

My dad poured the things in the box out on the splintery floorboards. There was a silver dollar and some marbles and a nugget that looked like gold but was really brass, and there was that flint point. He picked it up and rubbed the broken back corner with his thumb. He's got the roughest thumbs you ever saw, with cracked nails and cuts about half healed and old stickery scars he got doing hard work.

"Where'd you get the arrowhead?" I asked.

He nodded toward the hay door and said: "About twenty miles that way as the crow flies, but lots farther the crooked way we had to walk." I squinted my eyes against sun to look out. We were way high above the valley. The woods were black and brown and bare already. I could see the river rapids shining up that way and more woods and some low hills. Then, far away, a jaggedy line of high hills where the land met the blue sky.

"Where did you walk?"

He said it was up that same stream, the North Fork of the White River, and after that a long ways east up something called Bear Creek. They finally got to a mountain which the map called the Three Sisters, but which they called the Three Stooges. It was one big mountain with three peaks that rose up sharp like cliffs. Two of them were brushy, but the one to the south was flat on top and bare.

"We figured that one must be Curly," my dad said, "and the other two were Moe and Larry."

"We?" I said. "You told me *we* played on the sawhorses, and *we* smoked cigarettes. Who was this *we?*"

He took my cigarette and his and mashed the fire end of both under his horny old thumb, like nothing could hurt it worse anyhow.

He said: "After this, you kick my rear if you catch me smoking, and I'll kick yours the same way. Deal?"

"You didn't answer," I told him. "Who is the *we?*" He quit smiling as the last streak of smoke disappeared.

"Me and Emmett Corvin," he said.

I knew they named me after Emmett Corvin. I knew Emmett was the one who got to be a pilot, but that's all I knew. Daddy would never talk about him. That time in the barn my dad must've been pretty zapped because he finally told me some of it.

"Emmett was just a great kid. Right from the time we went to Tigris Grade School, all the kids knew he would be great. He was a true daredevil."

Daddy said the other boys dared Emmett one day, so he dove fifty feet from the bank into blue water in an old strip pit where they used to mine coal. The fifty feet down wasn't that hard. The hard part was, you had to run fast and fly far enough out to reach over the sloping bank to deep water. Emmett did it all right, but my dad followed and nearly killed himself on a rock. That's how he lost that half of his ear.

"You lied to me," I said. "You always told me Mama bit that ear off."

"Did you believe it?"

"Heck, no."

"Then I didn't lie. I just didn't want you finding out I was dumb enough to dive fifty feet without any water under me."

One bad ear didn't stop my dad from going around with Emmett Corvin. They saved up and bought pack frames and a Navy surplus rubber raft and two great long Navy sheath knives. They were going to carry everything up to the head of Bear Creek. Then they would blow the raft up with air and float back down. See, nobody had ever floated it before, nobody Emmett or Daddy had heard of. They were going to be first.

The second evening out, they opened a package of bacon to cook for supper. They went up the creek to fish, and coming back, they heard this spooky sound like "Unk-unk-unk . . . ork-ork." It scared them.

Slowly they crept up close to their camp and saw— guess what? Hogs. Five big razorback hogs and a dozen pigs were rooting over their camp. Down in the Ozarks, some hogs have gone clean wild. They're skinny but get real big and old, with bristly skin and long yellow tusks. They live on acorns and whatever else they root out, like stuff that belongs to campers.

One boar hog had finished off the cardboard wrapper and was sucking down raw bacon strips like spaghetti. That was too much for my dad.

"You stupid cannibal!" he yelled.

The boys ran in and kicked at the hogs. Them razor-backs bristled all over and snorted and came after them with their tusks. A sow with pigs chased them up a cedar stump. She was so hot after them they couldn't even get to a decent tree.

Then the hogs stood in the camp and finished off all the food. They ate the marshmallows with the plastic sack they came in. Even the flour and sugar were gone except for white dust in the grass. The hogs walked around burping awhile and one boar took a leak. Then they just casually sauntered off in the woods. When my dad told me that, I laughed.

"It wasn't funny, son," he said.

But he laughed, too. After the razorbacks, they had to live off the land. It was nothing but crawdad tails and goggle-eye perch and the roots of some cattails. Once they caught a four-pound blue catfish. Took 'em two more days to get up to Three Stooges, but they had fun there.

They found big overhangs of rock like caves and carved their initials where other names were already carved. Maybe Emmett and Daddy were the first to float Bear Creek, but they weren't the first people to walk up there—not by a long shot.

Emmett found four good lance points under the over-hangs. Daddy found just that one point, in what looked to be old-time trash heaps where Indians threw stuff away. They camped in a rock shelter on Curly and built a big fire, then watched the sun go down over mountains to the west.

"We talked about what we would do with our lives. We were gonna get in ROTC at some college. Then we'd maybe be Navy pilots and fly Phantom jets. The Vietnam War was big then. We'd be war aces, see, and then maybe we'd be astronauts and go to the moon. The least we'd do is go to Alaska and be bush pilots. We'd land airplanes on mountains and maybe fly to the North Pole." Daddy shook his head. "I never blabbed so much nonsense, and I never had such a good time."

The next day they blew up their rubber raft and found out why nobody ever floated Bear Creek before. There wasn't enough water. They kept scraping bottom and carrying the raft till they were wore out. Took two days to go about three miles. Then a big rain came, the water rose up, and away they went.

"The creek looked dangerous," my dad said, "but it wasn't—all except one place, and even that place didn't look dangerous to Emmett."

Just before Bear Creek ran into the North Fork of the White River, the creek bed tilted to the right in this long white-water rapid. The water crowded to the right and rushed into a deep pool. Looking at it from the top of the rapid, my dad could see the pool was jammed with brush.

Daddy told Emmett they should carry the boat and other stuff around that dangerous place. He picked up his and Emmett's packs and started walking downstream beside the rapids. Next thing, here comes Emmett riding down the fast water. He stood on the floating canvas bottom of the raft with his hands raised high, yelling that Daddy was chicken.

The raft bumped over a slick rock that suddenly pooched up the canvas bottom and booted Emmett in the water. Daddy said it looked like the boat just spat him out. The boat whirled around the brush and went downstream, but Emmett sank in the swift current. Daddy ran down the creek and then back, watching for Emmett to come up. He didn't come up.

Then my dad jumped out on the honey-locust brush jammed in the pool. It was full of these terrible thorns that honey locusts have. He walked on branches till he was way over the water. The branches sank in till he was hip deep. He got stabbed about a hundred times by thorns, and the current washed away his blood.

He looked down in the clear water. There was Emmett, struggling real weak to get up through brush. Emmett's mouth was open like he was yelling. All my dad heard was the roar of the rapids. One locust branch was holding the brush and Emmett down.

Daddy yanked out his Navy knife and started chopping. He hacked and cut and panted like crazy till the branch snapped and went down with the current. Emmett almost went with it. Daddy caught Emmett's shirt and dragged him up. Emmett could barely cough the water out and make a sucking noise for air.

"Huuuuuuuuuuhhhnnn. . ."

Daddy dragged him across the brush and up on the bank. Emmett just lay there breathing for a long time. He was bloody from my dad's own blood. My dad said he thought they should be blood brothers from then on, because all of a sudden he liked Emmett more than ever before.

But it wasn't that way with Emmett.

"Why'd you have to tear my shirt?" he said. Daddy didn't answer him back. Pretty soon Emmett said: "Ain't you got me bloody enough? Don't stand right where it drips on me.

So Daddy moved away. After a while Emmett said: "It never would've happened, see, if you hadn't chickened out. If you'd rode down with me, that never would've happened."

After my dad told me that, he got real quiet again, but I didn't.

"Why did he say that? You saved his life."

"No, I didn't. He would've got out of that one, too. Emmett always came out of scrapes okay."

Daddy said they found the raft caught on some rocks below and rode it home that same day. When I asked what happened to Emmett after their trip, he said Emmett ended up doing most of what they talked about up on Curly. He went to college and got in ROTC. He flew airplanes for the Navy and after that he flew helicopters, but he never went to Alaska.

"What happened to you?" I asked my dad.

"You know what happened to me." He smiled at his shoes. "I married your mother and quit Ava High School so I could get a full-time job."

"What happened to Emmett Corvin?"

"I already told you."

"I mean now. Where is Emmett now?"

"He disappeared" is all my dad answered.

"Disappeared? You mean he flew off somewhere in an airplane and was never found again?"

"No."

"What happened to him?"

"He disappeared." Daddy stood up to brush the hay off his jeans. "We better get them tools and stuff loaded for the drive home."

Still, he didn't go anywhere. He stood quiet for a minute looking out the hay door, the same way he stands by the airstrip watching the planes go up. This time he wasn't smiling. I knew he couldn't see the three-topped mountain where they built their campfire. A jaggedy line of hills was in between, and lots of misty sky. But that's where my dad was looking—toward the mountain.

10

I WONDERED IF I could find the creek and the mountain and the mastodon hunters' cave on the airplane map behind the seat. I asked Essie to get it for me. The map was coming apart at the folds. The old man who owned the Taylorcraft had patched it with Scotch tape, which was blistered and scaly like sunburned skin. The paper was so worn it felt like a dollar bill you'd kept in your pocket about a hundred years.

"Essie, hold the yoke. I need to look at the map."

"I don't know how to fly an airplane."

"Neither do I. It's just like the handlebars on our bike, only it pulls to the left a little. Keep the wings level. Keep the nose on the horizon."

"What's the horizon?"

"You know what it is."

But I pointed at the hazy line where the highway met blue sky. We were crawling ever so slow toward it, with green country creeping past underneath. Up high like that, it seemed slow, even if we were passing every car on the highway.

"I see the school buses," Essie said.

I could see them, too. We always saw them on the way to Grandma's house, a bunch of yellow buses parked in a lot to the left of the highway. Essie took hold of the yoke on her side. Then I spread the map out on my knees.

There were circles on it and funny triangles I didn't understand. I could find where we were on Highway 71, I could find the North Fork of the White River all right, but no Three Stooges mountain, or even Three Sisters. Between us and there, it was just a big tangle of roads and rivers. The Three Stooges was just something my dad remembered from when he was a boy. I didn't see how we could ever find it, unless I followed the roads to Grandma's house.

The plane felt fine to me. But when I looked up from the map, the ground was tilted crazy below us. The left wing and the nose were down. We were slipping sideways and down. Essie sat with her eyes wide, squeezing the yoke so hard her fingers were white.

"Look out, you doggone dumbbell!" I hollered. She let go and jumped back against the seat. I grabbed the yoke on my side and twisted to the right—too far, I guess, because the right wing sank low and we started sliding in that direction.

"Emmett, be careful!"

This time I moved the yoke slow till the Taylorcraft straightened up and the nose came even with the horizon. We just sat there breathing long breaths.

"Me be careful?" I said. "After what you did?"

"It's not like you said," she told me. "It's not like the handlebars on the bike."

I didn't go on at her anymore. I was just glad I had flown twice before, with Billy and Mr. Teegarten, because I had learned a little.

"We got to turn on Highway 7," I said.

"That's no skin off my nose."

I guess I knew the real true Highway 7 wouldn't be blue like it was on the map, but I flew right past it. I had to turn north and east before we hit it—just a gray concrete road like the rest of them.

Then I nearly did it again, nearly missed another turn to a different highway. I twisted the yoke a little, and the ailerons on the wings put us in a bank to the right. Without even using the rudder, we started turning to line up on Highway 13. This time I kept looking at the ground below and thinking it couldn't be real. I couldn't believe that the seat and the wood floor of the cabin were the only things holding us up. The more I looked down, the weirder I felt. It was like a dream or a nightmare where you fall and fall and never hit the ground.

"Cut it out," I said.

"Cut what out?"

"I was talking to myself."

I stopped looking down and looked at the horizon long enough to straighten us out over Highway 13. Then I looked at the instruments. They still said RPM, MPH, CLIMB, CARBURETOR HEAT, PRIMER. I couldn't remember what Daddy said they meant, but it didn't matter, because none of them worked anyhow. The only thing that worked was the compass that hung right above the control panel. It pointed southeast, which was the way we wanted to go.

Then the highway went across a bridge over a big lake. The lake wasn't on the map, but I remembered it from trips to Grandma's house. We were finding our way, all right. I saw motorboats and water skiers going fast and a houseboat that left a white V on the water. Even looking down, I was starting to feel better, till I saw Essie was doing the same thing—looking at all that wet water.

"Emmett," she said. "Emmett, I got to go."

Go? I didn't know where she was going to go. "Essie, there ain't no bathroom up here."

"I got to go." She jiggled her feet up and down on the floor of the cabin. I didn't say anything. I just held my breath a while and stared at the little clouds ahead. Pretty soon we were away from the water and over green land. I figured that might help her, but then we came to another lake.

"*Emmmmmm*-mett!"

"Essie, I don't know . . ."

She started jiggling her feet again. "Well, you better find out quick."

"Okay, Essie. All right," I said, and grinned at her. I reached to the toolbox behind the seat and found a coffee can full of nails. I poured the nails in the bottom of the box and gave the can to her.

"Here."

"Here, *what?*" she said.

"Do it in that."

"You want me to do it right in front of *you?*"

"No," I yelled, "I want you to crawl out on the end of the wing!"

I like to never got her to pee. She kept yelling at me to look the other way, like she had something I was just dying to see. I changed her diaper lots when she was little. That's when I saw more of Essie than I ever want to see again. She finally did it in the can. I slid the window back and poured it out on my side. After the guinea goo and the guinea crap, that's all the Taylorcraft needed.

We kept flying on. Once we saw a silver airplane, looked to me like a twin, flying crosswise to us way ahead, sliding like a fish through the air. That's how the air looks when you're flying, like a giant aquarium, and you're just one of its fish. We came swimming up fast behind a raggedy line of white geese. They broke off when the plane came close.

Then I started worrying that we were going too fast, that the engine would strain itself, running flat out that way, or the wind over the wings would tear the fabric worse. My dad had been able to control the gas at the carburetor when he was working on the engine, so he didn't need the throttle. But I couldn't climb out now and get under the cowling to reach the carburetor.

"Essie, I got to fix that throttle. We can't be going this fast when we come down. You're going to have to hold the yoke again."

She sat back in the seat and put her hands down to her sides. "I can't. I'll crash us."

I had to argue five minutes before she'd try it. Even then, she made me promise I wouldn't call her a dumbbell again. After that, she reached out and took the yoke.

"It'll pull to the left," I told her. "You got to pull it back."

I leaned over and got some spray oil and a pair of pliers out of my dad's toolbox. I squirted it where the throttle rod went into the control panel. Then I squeezed myself down and reached behind to spray the rod from the back side where it came out of the panel. I twisted the knob with the pliers. I pounded and jerked. It wouldn't work.

"Yaaaaaaaa!" Essie yelled. "We're crashing!"

I raised my head and saw the horizon slanting crazy again, with the plane tilting and diving down to the left and a big silo made out of red tile coming up at us. I jumped back in the seat and grabbed the yoke on my side. This time she didn't let go of hers.

"Turn it loose, you idiot!"

"I'm gonna hang on!" she yelled back. "I'm gonna learn it!" At least she didn't fight me for the controls. She just held on to feel what I was doing as I twisted the yoke to work the ailerons, then slowly pulled it back to bring us out of the dive. We were flying level, with the silo way behind us, when she said: "You called me an idiot."

"Well, I didn't call you a dumbbell."

She sat back in her seat and looked straight ahead, with her teeth clenched. "You just watch," she said. "I'm going to learn it."

She was pretty dumb, but she finally did seem to learn it. I said, "Okay, I got to unstick the throttle. But this time don't look down. Keep watching the horizon. Keep that left wing up."

I had already sprayed where the throttle rod went through the control panel. This time I bent down and sprayed oil where the rod went through the fire wall from the cabin to the engine compartment. Then I popped my head up quick to see if we were crashing.

Essie had leaned her body way to the right, like she thought that would keep the plane straight. And the plane was straight. The wings were level. I ducked under and sprayed again and wiggled and twisted the rod. I could feel it come loose. I sat up and jerked the knob out a little at a time. The engine calmed down and the wing fabric didn't flap so hard.

"Oh, boy," I said, "ain't that better?"

Essie was leaning to the right and grinning. "I can fly better than you," she said.

I was surprised she gave the controls back to me so easy.

11

I NOTICED THE sun was getting low in the west. I wondered would we make it to our hideout before dark. I didn't know how we were going to land anyway, and we sure couldn't get down alive after dark.

The ground below us got hillier and woodsier, and there weren't so many cornfields. We saw Springfield just where it was supposed to be on the map. We saw the freeway that we drove the station wagon on around the city toward Grandma's house, but the freeway wasn't on the map, either. I figured the map was so old that the lake and freeways weren't even built then. But it turned out to be easy just from memory to find Highway 60, which Daddy always followed east toward Mountain Grove. I thought we had it made, when all of a sudden the engine said, "Brrrrrrrrp!"

For a while it sounded smooth again, like "Rrrrrr-rr. . ." Then it said, "Brrrp! Brrrp!" We pitched forward in our seats, the Taylorcraft slowed so much. The nose tilted down. Then the engine started again: "Rrrrrrrrrrr . . ." Essie's eyes were about like fried eggs looking at me.

"What's wrong?" she asked.

"I don't know."

But I did know we hadn't gone any six hours and we hadn't flown any five hundred miles. We couldn't be out of gas. The engine said, "Brrrp! Brrrrrp!

Brrrrrrrrp!" I could feel the plane get weak underneath and start to sink. I looked down at telephone poles and silos sticking up and the barbed-wire fences. The engine caught for a minute, then went, "Brrp! Brrp! Brrrrrrrrrrrrp!" Essie yelled into my face: "It happened like that in the station wagon when Mama ran out of gas."

"Brrrp! Brrrrrrrrrp! Brp!"

I grabbed above her head for the lever that said, FILL MAIN TANK IN LEVEL FLIGHT ONLY. I grabbed and slapped it over from off to on. Then I reached over my head and did the lever on my side.

"Brp! Brrrrrp! Brrrrrrrrrrrrr . . ." the engine said, and it kept on breathing easy like that. We had plenty of gas all right, but it wasn't doing any good in the auxiliary tanks. So Wrong-Way Ragsdale nearly killed us again by doing something dumb. That started me thinking how much I am like Jimmy Doolittle, who has always been my favorite hero.

Once, just for fun, Jimmy dove his old Army biplane to scare an American soldier walking on a road. The soldier didn't even duck or act scared, which made Jimmy mad. He figured next try he would zoom low enough to scare the soldier, and Jimmy did. His rubber airplane tire clunked the soldier on the head, which is just the start of the dumb stuff he did in a book I read about hero pilots.

Because then Jimmy's plane kept on swooping down so low the wheels hooked on a wire fence. The wire didn't break but stretched out like a tennis net with the posts yanking out and the staples popping till Jimmy Doolittle was standing still in the air. Then, *bammo*, he fell about ten feet straight down and smacked up a ten-thousand-dollar airplane.

Jimmy ran back to help the guy on the road. Lucky

thing, the soldier was only knocked out cold and woke up quick. But I figure Jimmy must've felt pretty dumb about it. Still, he went on and became the best pilot in the world and flew B-25 bombers better than anybody in World War II. Jimmy Doolittle always came through, and maybe I could, too, as long as I had Essie to remind me of things.

She was sitting with her hands in her lap, looking straight ahead through the propeller.

"See," she said. "See, Emmett."

Essie was telling me she could be smart, too, she could be useful. "See," she said, and that's all she said. She didn't push it on me. She didn't rub my nose in it. All of a sudden she looked cute to me, so I patted her dishwater dumb-blond head.

"Yeeeeg!" she yelled and slapped my hand away.

After a while I saw a water tower that said Mountain Grove on the side. It was on the west side of the town and south of the big highway we were following. We were getting close to the hideout. I turned and went south over town. I flew right over the Brown Shoe Company, where my Uncle Aaron Ragsdale works.

From there, the road went into hills and got too twisty to follow. I hit straight south by the compass, figuring we were bound to cross the North Fork of the White River. The country had been woodsy before. Now it got rougher yet, with the hills rising up under us. The trees just whizzed past underneath, but we didn't see the North Fork. First thing you know, here was a sliver of blue water between the hills that widened slowly out. It was another one of the lakes. By then, I needed to go pretty bad myself. I didn't need any more lakes of wet water.

I figured the river must run in where the lake started, so we turned and went back. Sure enough, we had missed it on the first pass because it was hidden by trees. This time I saw it and followed upstream where it ran beside a gravel country road. Right where the gravel road turned into dirt, there was an old barn that had got tired and leaned over on its side. And I knew where I was. I knew exactly.

"Hey, Essie, that's the North Fork. Watch for Grandma's house."

I came down lower. The ground raced under us, mostly woods and pasture, with a couple of plowed fields in the bottomland. Then there was just woods and pasture. In a minute we saw it, a tin-roofed house and a gray wood barn not half as big as the one that got tired. When I was little, I thought Grandpa's barn belonged to a giant. Now it looked like a barn for Essie's stuffed animals.

Right beside it stood a man, who I figured must be Alva Cody, the friend of my dad's who bought the farm at the auction. He shaded his eyes from the sun to look at us, and the black shadow of the Taylorcraft went across him. He didn't even duck. I turned in a wide circle and went over again.

"Hey," Essie said, "that man sees us. I thought we were going to hide out."

I didn't know why I went over the second time either, so I didn't answer. I just headed out over Granddad's north pasture, which was the last pasture, then over woods and on up the valley, following the North Fork.

"Look," Essie said.

She was pointing out her side to a mountain way higher than the Taylorcraft. Pretty soon I saw one like that on my side. Mountains started humping up around us. They weren't big and snowy like pictures I've seen of Colorado, but they looked very big when you flew under them. It was like something way beneath the ground was moving and pushing up the hills that way. Maybe it was the old-time mastodons the Indians hunted, trying to bust up through the skin of the woods.

The next thing I had to find was Bear Creek. We flew over two creeks coming from the east, and I worried that one of them was it. Then we came to a third creek, with a long white-water rapid, where the current rushed to the right side into a deep pool just before it ran into the North Fork. And I knew we were there. I knew it from my dad's story. All by itself, the plane turned and went up Bear Creek.

I couldn't believe it. I couldn't believe we had got through the snarly tangle of roads and rivers from home to here. That's when I figured out you don't have to know all the way to some far place before you start. All you have to find is the first place on the way, and then the next one, then the one after that. Pretty soon you're there.

We came around the curve of the creek between some low hills. Straight ahead was a mountain bigger than any of them. The sun was so far down in the sky it didn't shine on the mountain, which was black, but it did shine on some pink clouds high up and even on some hawks or eagles.

The hawks hung still in the air with their wings out and tip feathers spread like fingers on the wind. The black mountain stuck up from a long ridge. It looked like somebody threw an army tent over the biggest mastodon of them all. I could see his shoulder through it and the bulgy muscles in his back. Just to make him mad, somebody had set three pillbox hats on his slanty forehead. Two of them were furry with brush, but the one to the south was bare. He was struggling mad as the devil under the tent, trying to push up.

So we were here, for whatever good that would do. I

began to see how dumb I had been, taking this airplane, and how everything I did after that was worse. I took us to the loneliest place in three hundred miles, without any open pasture to land in. But we had to come down before it got dark. We had to.

How do you land a plane in woods a hundred feet deep when you're busting to go to the bathroom?

12

ESSIE HELD THE yoke again while I did it in the coffee can. She flew us north along that ridge, all the time trying to look over at me.

"Cut it out, Essie!"

"Who cares about that?" she said.

"I care! You stop it!"

She stopped looking, and I got the job done. Wheeeew. Then I poured it out the window and turned us south again. When we turned, we slowed down a lot. I could see that by watching the ground. There was a strong wind blowing against us from the south. All along that ridge, the hawks were riding it. They were black like the mountain now, and the clouds were gray, because the sun was gone. We had to get down fast. I pulled out the throttle to slow us more and tried to remember what Tom Weldon said about how he landed in woods once after his engine stopped.

He glided low and sort of pancaked into trees. It tore the plane up, Tom said, but if you do it right, woods are second best to pastures for keeping people alive. He also said the seat belt saved him, which reminded me that all this way we should've been wearing belts. I quick told Essie to buckle up.

"I won't, either," she told me. "You don't ever buckle up without Daddy making you."

"He does, though. He makes me, and I do it."

I buckled my belt to show her I could without anybody making me. That belt was dirty, but it was a good wide one, made out of heavy canvas. Essie just looked mean at me.

"Buckle the belt!" I told her.

"I am not the slave of you," she said.

Boy, she made me mad. I hated her. It would be my fault if she got hurt, and everybody would be all the madder at me. I tapped the round altimeter gauge in front of her face.

"Without the seat belt, Essie, that's right where your head will hit. The control panel will be covered with blood and brains, if you got any brains. After we crash, I'll be about ankle deep in your blood and pasty brains."

She didn't look mean after that. Her chin turned trembly. Tears popped out in her eyes and ran down out of her nose.

"Don't scare me, Emmett. Please, please, don't scare me."

Her eyes got red, and her mouth pulled down like a tragedy. She was so choked she couldn't breathe right. With Essie I always say the wrong thing. I always do wrong with her. I wanted to bang my own head on the altimeter. Why can't I ever do her right? Anyhow, she let me help her buckle up.

The mountain stood high to the left and ahead, with a dozen hawks riding the wind in front. They were so still it looked like somebody had hung 'em up on hooks. The wind they were riding ruffled the trees in the woods. I looked at the trees and started getting scared. They were black-green and then white-green when a gust turned the leaves up.

We were flying into the wind, which is the way they always land planes on the airstrip back home. That's the way Jimmy Doolittle would try it. In his life, he crashed a dozen times and he bailed out in a parachute three times. He didn't get killed because he did it right. I pulled out the throttle knob, and we sank. Tree branches started reaching up for us.

I didn't want to sink, and neither did Essie. She breathed through her mouth and cried some more.

"Emmett, I'm scared!"

"Hush up," I told her. "You're gonna scare me, too." I was already scared, but I had to keep watching. I had to do right.

Essie grabbed my shoulder with both hands. "I'm scared, Emmett."

"Hush up."

And she did. She looked straight ahead and clamped her mouth shut. I pulled the throttle to slow down a little more. The branches of one tall sycamore stuck up high from the rest of the woods. I tapped the rudder to go around that tree.

Then, way ahead, the leaves turned white in a gust of wind. The whiteness in the leaves came rushing toward us like a wave. A hawk high above got blown back. He had to flap his wings. The wind hit us and we lifted a little. The tall sycamore stood nearly still beside us. I yanked the throttle all the way out. The propeller spun down and stopped. It was quiet. Good gosh, it was quiet. All I could hear was the wind on the wings and our own loud breathing.

"Jimmy Doolittle," I said. I don't know why I said it. "Jimmy Doolittle, Jimmy Doolittle."

Maybe I did everything wrong, maybe I did it stupid, but there wasn't anything more I could do now. I was glad. We sank straight down.

Essie said: "O-o-o-o-o-o-o-o. . ."

She still had her fingers digging into my shoulder. Then *crash*, the Taylorcraft tilted one way, and *crash*, the nose tilted up, *rip* and *tear*, and it tilted down again. The stub of a branch poked in through the window on my side. There was sharp glass on my lap. Then we tilted to the right and fell off the stub.

The wing struts popped loud. The wings folded straight above us like the wings of a hawk when it's diving. The air way high is like an aquarium you fly through, but the woods are a dark ocean. We fell down and down, *crash* and *bash* and *rip* and *tear* I saw blood on my left arm and wondered where it came from. We fell and bounced and bumped. It got darker and greener like the bottom of the sea. Then everything stopped.

"Jimmy Doolittle," I said again.

I heard loud breathing, like in the locker room at De Soto Junior High when the basketball team comes in from practice. The plane was tilted sideways, so I had to look down at Essie. Her eyeballs shined in the light. Her mouth was just a red smear.

"Oh, God, oh God, Essie."

I reached out for her, but she smacked my hand.

"Don't!" She put both hands up to feel her face. "It's my tooth. I knocked out a tooth." She held the tooth up in bloody fingers. "It's just a baby tooth." She nodded to the control panel. There was red blood on the altimeter. "See, I hit it anyway. You're bleeding, too."

There was a gash on my arm below the left sleeve.

"It's okay," I told her. "It don't hurt." But it did.

That stub had smashed the door on my side. The door wouldn't open, and it was above me anyway. I reached over and turned the handle on Essie's door. It fell wide open.

"Don't!" she yelled.

"You're not gonna fall. You got your seat belt on." The ground was maybe eight feet below, just dead leaves with white toadstools sticking up. I unbuckled, then crawled across Essie and held the doorframe with my hands and dropped on the soft ground, old leaves piled up for years and rotted. Essie threw down her big purse and came down the same way. I caught her when she dropped. I could catch her easy when she was little, but this time she knocked me down.

I didn't get up. Essie got up, but I didn't. I just lay there on the ground like an old-time helmet diver lying on the floor of the ocean, with light coming down through deep water. I looked up and saw how the branches closed behind us, the way water closes over a sinking ship. Through the leaves I saw the sky, still blue but dark enough already so some stars were shining. Essie stood over me, wiping tears out of her eyes.

"Get up, Emmett. Why don't you get up?"

"I will," I told her, but I didn't.

Over our heads, my dad's Taylorcraft was caught in a low crotch of this great huge bur oak. It looked terrible. Once in our yard in De Soto I saw a blue jay catch a fat grasshopper and crunch him good and then spit him out in the lilac bush, because he tasted lousy. Our airplane looked like the grasshopper, with the wings bent up, the fuselage split open, the tail broke off, the fabric ripped and torn. The yellow rope was still hanging from the tail wheel.

Then I remembered something like a clear picture in my head, like I was seeing myself do it again. Before I even crawled in the Taylorcraft, the first thing I did was take the rope off the hangar post it was looped around. Otherwise, the rope would've stopped the plane.

That's when I figured out that I did more than just push in the throttle of the Taylorcraft. I did more than just make people *think* I stole a plane. I *stole* it. I really did. I stole that airplane and wrecked it and someday the police would catch me.

"Are you sick, Emmett?" Essie asked. Why don't you get up?"

"I will," I told her.

But I didn't get up. All I wanted was to lie there, and I didn't even want that very much. The branches above me waved in the wind, and the wind said, "Whoo-oo-oo-ooo. . ." The night got darker, and the wind kept on. Essie already had blood on the front of her hands.

Now she stood there in the leaves wiping the fresh tears away with her knuckles and getting blood on them, too. That's when she said the worst thing she could've said, the thing that made me feel the rottenest. She took a big long shuddery breath.

"I want my mama," she said. "Oh, Emmett, I want my mama."

I wanted her, too. I wanted my mom, but I wanted my dad even more.

13

I FIGURED I would keep lying on the soft ground
and after a while just die. It would be less trouble than
getting up. Essie kept breathing and shuddering and
finally gasped out: "*Emmmmmmm*-mett. I'm thirsty."

I was thirsty, too. My mouth was so dry the spit was
sticky. I got up. By then, my eyes were used to the
dark. I could see pretty well. We walked downhill a
ways and found a trickle of water from a spring. That
country's full of springs.

I held a double handful of water against the sky and
watched it drip. The water was clear, so we drank. It
tasted like iron. Still, it was good. We washed the blood
off ourselves and walked back to the plane. Essie put
her left arm around me and tucked her head under my
arm and clung tight to me as we walked. That was the
first time she ever did such a thing. I didn't mind it too
much.

We were hungry, but I didn't know where we could
find anything to eat. I was sleepy, too. We both lay
down on the soft leaves. Essie kept breathing real shuddery, like she would never get over it. I felt guilty because I got her in this and because never never in my
whole life did I ever do Essie right.

When she was born, see, my family was having a hard
time. Mama just barely brought Essie home from the
hospital when my dad got terrible pains in his gut and

had to have his appendix cut out. So there was Essie and Ethel still in diapers and Evelyn just big enough to walk around fast but not smart enough to stay away from the second-story stairs.

It was just me and Mom to take care of the kids, and Mom was white as a sheet for three weeks after she brought Essie home. I didn't see how there could be that many dirty diapers in the world. I would get one changed and, phhhlllp, Essie would fill up the fresh one. Mama would sit in the living room all sick and ragged out from housework.

"Good old Emmett, Big Sister Emmett," she'd say. "You're a wonderful Big Sister."

But I wasn't. I was lousy and mean, especially to Essie, who was littlest and way the most trouble. It wasn't her fault. I knew that, but I blamed her anyway. Lots of times she'd get to bawling so excited she wouldn't take her bottle. I would slap the bed on both sides real loud to startle her quiet, then stuff the nipple in before she could start again. At two o'clock in the morning it would be just the opposite. Then she'd take about an ounce of milk and fall asleep and wake up hungry an hour later.

Between times I never even got to sleep. I started shaking her to keep her awake so she could get the whole four ounces at once. I shook her so hard her teeth would rattle, if she'd had any teeth. Once I took hold of her red feet and held her upside down till she got scared all of a sudden and woke up screaming.

I never told anybody this before, how mean I was to her, but I was mean. Essie never liked me after that. I didn't like her even as much as she liked me. All I ever felt about her was guilty, which is what I felt that night in the woods, listening to her shudder and shudder as she breathed.

Suddenly she caught her breath and said: "My tooth hurts, Emmett."

"I'm sorry."

"I still got the tooth in my pocket. There isn't really a tooth fairy. I don't believe that anymore."

I didn't know what she wanted me to say.

"I just wish we had a pillow to put it under," I told her.

The leaves crinkled under my left ear, and leaves were creeping under my shirt collar. Leaves give you the itches, they make a lousy bed unless you've got a blanket to lay over them.

"Emmett, what do you reckon Mama and Daddy are doing?"

There was a white toadstool growing between me and Essie. I could see gills on the bottomside of the toadstool and a bug hanging underneath and Essie's beady eyes shining on the other side.

"I want to know, Emmett. I want to know what they're doing."

"Well," I said, "I guess Mama would be cleaning up after supper. She cooked chicken the way Grandma used to in the oven, no wings, just chicken backs this time with real crisp skin. Now she's looking in the living room to see what Daddy's watching on TV. All the kids are in there, too. They're supposed to be watching TV, but Ethel and Robert aren't. Ethel is playing cards with herself like she does, laying them out on the floor. Robert picks one up and turns it over. Ethel says, 'Stop it, Robert!' And he says, 'They're my cards, too!' "

Under the toadstool I saw Essie smile a little bit and rub her eyes.

"What does Mama say to them?"

"She doesn't say anything to them. She goes over and stands behind Daddy's chair and puts her hands on his shoulders. Then he reaches up and pats her on the arm. That's what they're doing."

"I see," Essie said, and she smiled again.

But I didn't believe what I told her. I thought our mom and dad would be running around in the car or calling on the telephone, trying to find us. They might be blaming each other for the wrong thing I did and fighting about it. My dad might be standing out beside the airstrip like he does, watching the planes with their beacon lights blinking and their landing lights shining ahead. He might be remembering how our plane took off and never came back.

Essie said: "Tell me a story about Mama and Daddy."

"Okay," I said, "but the only one I can think of has me in it, too. It isn't even a story."

She scritched her way closer through the leaves so her face was almost under the toadstool, looking across at me. "Tell it."

"Well, I was a tiny kid then, way littler than you are now. We would all be coming home from somewhere at night in the car. We had a different car then. But Evelyn and Ethel would be sleeping in the back seat, so I was in front with Mom and Dad."

"Where was I?" Essie asked.

"You was just a gleam in Daddy's eye," I told her, because that's what my mom said to her lots of times. I know what it means, but Essie doesn't.

"Tell the story."

"When I got sleepy, they would stretch me out across the front seat, with my head in Daddy's lap and my feet in Mama's. I knew we were driving, but it was more like floating on a cloud. Mama would pat my legs with her hand. Sometimes Daddy would reach down and cup my head in his hand and squeeze me easy against his belly.

"His belt buckle was cold, but it felt good anyway. I would lie there and look straight out the window on Dad's side and see the stars in the sky standing still, even if we were driving fast. I knew nothing could hurt me there. I could go to sleep or stay awake, whichever one I wanted, and I would be safe."

Essie's mouth was open but her eyes were closed. She was almost asleep. By then I wasn't sleepy myself anymore. I just lay there and listened to the wind and watched through the trees when the moon rose in the east. From way up on Three Stooges came this crazy laughing sound—a bunch of stuttery yips and yowls. I'd heard it before at Grandpa's farm and even around our place in De Soto, and knew it was coyotes. Coyotes almost never hurt people, my dad says. I got up anyhow and broke off a dead branch for a club, then went back and lay down by Essie. It looked like the stars were standing still in the sky above us, the way they did in the car with Mom and Dad.

I still remembered how good it felt. That long time ago, I thought things would always stand still like the stars. Mom and Dad and me would go on forever the same way. But they got more and more kids till I was only one in six, and everything else changed, too. Even the stars don't really stand still. When you grow up, you got to grow out of that.

14

MY STOMACH STARTED talking to me next morning. It went, "Grug-lug." That's what woke me up. I opened my eyes and saw a sky above the trees that looked like a quilted comforter, long sausage clouds with blue sky between. The sun was up just enough to turn the clouds pink. I hadn't had one bite of food since Mama served me dinner the day before. I was hungry.

I started thinking here I was a man and pretty tough besides. So if I was that hungry, how hungry would little Essie be? I had dragged the poor kid three hundred miles to this wilderness, and she wanted her mama. She wasn't going to find her mama. On top of it, she had to go hungry. I decided to let her sleep so she wouldn't have to feel the hunger like I was.

Imagine my surprise when I turned over and saw there was just a hollow in the brown leaves where she'd been sleeping. She was already awake. Not only that, she was taking her ease on a mossy rock just up the slope. Not only that, poor Little Orphan Essie was munching her way like Pac-Man through a Hershey's Big Block candy bar.

"Where did you get *that*?" I asked.

"I don't know," she said. "Maybe the tooth fairy gave it to me."

I walked up to see it close. The brown chocolate was melting in her pink mouth, and the almonds said *crunch-crunch* between her teeth. With almonds is my very favorite.

I said: "That's what happened to Mama's box of Hershey Big Blocks."

"Mama wouldn't mind," Essie said. "She would be glad I got it."

"Where's the rest of them?" I asked.

Essie just looped the strap of her purse up over her shoulder and crooked her arm tight around the purse.

"What else you got in there? I bet that's where the whole-wheat Fig Newtons went."

Essie poked in the last bite of chocolate and licked her sticky fingers. Way deep inside, my stomach mooed like a cow. I said: "Kids who steal food and hide it are afraid of the world. They're insecure, that's what Ann Landers says."

Essie didn't answer. Her tennis shoes were jiggle-jiggling in the leaves as she wiggled her toes real satisfied. I thought about grabbing her feet and holding her upside down and shaking till the Hershey's Big Block candy bars came showering out. But I was too grownup for that.

"I don't want none of that sweet stuff anyhow," I told her. "What I need is a healthy breakfast."

I walked away from her toward the sound of Bear Creek. It wasn't easy walking up and down little ridges and around the dead trees. That was all virgin timber through there, mostly tall black oak and hickory with some knobby-trunked hackberry trees. I ducked under a dead tree all covered with grapevines. Then I saw the line of white sycamore trunks where Bear Creek ran. It was little for a river but big for a creek, way too wide to jump across. The water was so clear I could see the rocks on the bottom, rusty-red rocks mainly but also lots of wedge-shaped black rocks sticking out of the sand.

I took off my tennis shoes and waded in. My muscles were sore from the crash, and the cut on my arm hurt. I figured I might as well get sore feet, too, while I was catching that four-pound blue catfish for my breakfast. I walked back and forth about an hour and squatted down to look under rocks, but no catfish jumped into my pocket.

After a while I noticed two brown whiskers sticking out from under a rock and gently moving. I leaned over to look under the rock sideways. There was a crawdad staring out at me with beady eyes that stood up from his head on stalks. They were a lot like Essie's eyes, only hers aren't on stalks.

When I tipped the rock over, the crawdad raised his pincers up at me and started backing off toward deep water. He was mostly green but was so big and old part of his shell had turned orange and crusted over with knobby stuff like the hackberry bark. I saw a lobster once at Billy Teegarten's house just waiting to be cooked. That's what crawdads look like, only they're way smaller. Bad as I wanted to eat him, that's just how bad he didn't want me to. I grabbed at him, and he grabbed at me, but the crawdad grabbed the meanest.

"Ouch! Ouch!"

He came clear out of the water and didn't let go till I shook him loose. Then he zipped away, swimming backward out to deep water. I had two red marks where he pinched me in the web between my thumb and fingers. Okay. All right. That got me mad.

I started turning over rocks and looking for crawdads. The second one tried the same trick, but I reached around and grabbed his body behind the pincers. Ha! I stuffed him in the pocket of my jeans and went after more. Pretty soon that sucker pinched my leg through the pocket. I took him out and yanked his head off, then

75

stuffed the tail back into my pocket. That's the last pinching he ever did.

The third one swam away instant when I turned his rock up. I kept turning rocks over and grabbing till I turned one and stopped just short of grabbing a skinny brown snake. The snake scared me silly and went whipping away up the bank. Me, I jerked back so quick I sat in the water. Then came a "Hee, hee, hee, hee. . ." from up on the bank. It was Essie, who had followed me to the creek.

"Go on now," I told her. "Eat your sickening sweet unhealthy old Hershey bars."

She didn't go, but she didn't laugh at me anymore. I kept on with the crawdad stuff all morning. I kept stepping on the wedge-shaped black rocks in the sand. They weren't as sharp as they looked, they didn't cut my feet, but they bruised me blue. I turned over the rusty-red rocks and grabbed at crawdads and got pinched, and every once in a while I caught one. Hard as crawdads were to grab without getting grabbed myself, I would hate to hunt grizzly bears like Lewis and Clark did.

One time six of their men sneaked up behind this big grizzly they wanted to eat and shot him. The bullets just livened the grizzly up and reminded him he was hungry. Here right handy were these six good things to eat. He chased the hunters off a cliff into the Missouri River and jumped right in after them. The grizzly figured a little water wouldn't spoil the taste. He chased them out of the river onto the bank. They kept shooting and shooting with their rifles. They finally got to eat him, instead of the other way around.

Crawdads are easier than grizzlies, I found out, but not that much easier. I got soaking wet and froze blue in the cold water. The sun was straight over my head, and I was wore slick as the rocks in the creek when I gave it up. All I had was five crawdad tails.

Essie and me walked back to the plane together. I crawled up the tree trunk and out on a branch to get Dad's toolbox, which we carried back to a little rise of ground beside a pool on Bear Creek. In the toolbox was a jar of matches my dad used to light his soldering torch. I popped one and stuck it in some leaves and kindling wood. The fire caught quick.

Then I peeled the green shells off the crawdad tails and stuck 'em on a stick like marshmallows to cook. The fire was boiling steam out of my wet jeans by the time the crawdad tails started hissing and dripping fat. I blew on the first one and pulled it off the stick. It was the crawdad that pinched me through my pocket. I ate that sucker.

"Hey, Essie," I said, "these are good. You want to try one?"

"Yuck."

She was wrong about that, because they were delicious. But by the time you peeled and cooked 'em, each one was about the size of an olive. My stomach was sad that it invited two hundred to the party and only five came. I figured if I started soon and worked till black dark, I might catch five more to eat for supper. Essie sat down on the other side of the fire, pawing in her purse for something to eat. I could hear the cellophane cookie wrappers and paper candy wrappers crinkle in there.

"Essie," I said, "how would you like to hear another story?"

"It's all the same to me," she said.

"Well, this one is from a book I read about Captain Eddie Rickenbacker. It's not about when he was a famous fighter pilot in the First War. It's about later, when Captain Eddie and five other guys crashed their Flying Fortress in the Pacific Ocean."

"That's a boring story," Essie said. She pulled out a Hershey's Big Block candy bar and just sat there with it in her hand. She wasn't even hungry enough to eat it.

"Anyhow," I said, "Captain Eddie and his friends pretty near starved to death, floating around week after week in these rubber rafts. One day Captain Eddie was sitting there half asleep with his hat pulled down over his eyes, when all of a sudden he felt bird feet heavy on his head. Slowly, slowly, he reached his hands up and grabbed. He caught a sea gull. It was Captain Eddie's sea gull, because he caught it, but then he cut it up in little pieces and shared it with his five buddies. He shared every bite."

"Yuck," Essie said.

"The best part is still coming, because they used the guts of the sea gull as bait and caught some fish, which Captain Eddie also divided, so they all had a share. He shared the fish, and they all thought raw fish meat was cool and delicious."

"Yuck. Yuck."

"Before it was over," I told her, "one guy died, but the other five lived twenty-four days on the ocean and were rescued, all because they shared. They shared every bite of the food."

Essie yawned big and started stripping the wrapper down like a banana peel on the Hershey's Big Block. Then she took a bite. Her white teeth with little saw edges bit right through the creamy chocolate. It was hard, hearing her munch them almonds.

I looked off toward the creek and said: "Essie, a Hershey's Big Block is a horrible thing. It will make you fat. It will give you sugar diabetes and rot your teeth so they turn black and fall out in your hand. It's got the same stuff as coffee, which makes you nervous. A Hershey's Big Block candy bar will give you acne and huge pus-y pimples about the size of your thumb."

Right then I heard a little whoosh, and a fresh Hershey's Big Block landed in my lap. My hands were shaking so bad I could hardly peel the wrapper down. My mouth was open for the first bite when Essie smiled at me.

"What do you say, Emmett?"

"I don't know."

"What do you say when somebody gives you something nice?"

"Thank you," I said, sweeter than the sweet sweet first bite of that Hershey's Big Block. "Oh, thank you, thank you, dear darling sister Essie."

15

THAT'S WHAT I had to put up with. Her purse was full of biscuits two weeks old and M&M's in trick-or-treat packets and whole-wheat Fig Newtons and candy orange slices and dried-up chunks of cheese and crumbs of about everything else. I said, "Please, Essie," and, "Thank you, oh, thank you, dear sister Essie," and she doled it out like Captain Eddie. Without that stuff, we would've been eating our rubber shoe soles. Even with it, we were plenty hungry.

The whole second day I went after crawdads. I bruised my feet worse on them black wedge rocks sticking up from the sand. I busted my butt all day and only caught eleven. This time, when I started roasting 'em, Essie decided they weren't so yucky after all. She ate six.

And the next morning the skin of her arms was rough and red with big white spots bumped up on it. That scared me a little, because we didn't have the medicine Daddy gives her in a shot. But the crawdads just made her itch, they didn't bother her breathing.

That day we found some cattails like my dad said he ate. I peeled one root and crunched down. It was like a crisp bite of cucumber. We ate some of those, and I even caught two goggle-eye perch.

The way I did that, see, I bent a nail from the toolbox into a hook and tied it to the cotton line from my dad's plumb bob. I cut a hickory pole and baited the hook with worms from under a rock. Right quick I caught two. They were gold and brown in patches and lots brighter than goggle-eye from muddy Kansas farm ponds. Those two were all I caught that day. I let Essie have them, because she eats fish at home and doesn't turn red. Myself, I stuck with crawdads.

I found out something about them, too. You can just tie the head of a crawdad on a string and drop it in the water. Pretty soon a live one will grab hold with his pincers and start nibbling like a cannibal, worse than a razorback hog after bacon. You don't even have to hook the crawdad. He is so dumb he'll hang on tight even when you're lifting him out on the bank. Then you drop his tail in your pocket and use the head to catch the next one.

That night we heard thunder far away. The sky flickered over there. We just lay in the leaves on that rise of ground by the creek, because there wasn't anyplace better to go. Didn't seem like the thunder was getting closer.

It was black dark there in the woods, then all of a sudden it was bright white, and Essie was white as an angel beside me with the scaredest look I ever saw on her face. "*Crack-boooooooom!*" The lightning struck a tree down the creek. Essie hung around my neck, bawling and squalling. Then it rained, it rained like anything. It wasn't a cold rain, it was warm, and it stopped about as quick as it started.

We kept lying there kind of miserable on the leaves. At least we didn't get muddy. After a while she asked me to help her get over the scare by telling a story.

I told her one about a brother who had too much to do taking care of his family. He was so busy he got mad at his baby sister and treated her cruel. Sometimes he scared her and shook her hard, and once he even held her upside down. Essie started blinking sleepy at me in the dark.

"The brother was mean because he was having a hard time," she said.

Then she yawned big. She thought it was another boring story, but it made me feel better.

I got to thinking about how much we'd learned. I knew all about crawdads and perch and even ticks. There were these black ticks smaller than a pencil eraser that dig into your skin. When you yank 'em out, the head stays behind and makes a red sore way worse than a chigger bite. We had gotten so we could feel the tick when he first started walking on us. We could curl up a forefinger and flip that sucker about ten feet, so he could start staggering around and looking for somebody easier to bite.

We learned some things, but here it was the third night and we had already run out of food in the purse. I wasn't raised in that country, I couldn't hustle food as good as Daddy and the other Emmett. I could never catch enough goggle-eye and crawdads. It made me think how Dad has to hustle. You work your butt off, you keep doing the same thing every day, and still you never get enough.

'Course, if you try something different, it might not work and that day you wouldn't even have crawdads and fish to eat. You would never catch up. Lots of people like my mom and dad get in that fix. They keep doing the same thing because they can't afford to try anything new. But I figured me and Essie had to try. Otherwise, we would starve.

16

THE NEXT MORNING we started walking up the mountain. It was hard. We crawled over dead timber and tangled grapevines, and we got stuck by thorny bushes. We tried to go around the tangled places, up and down over little hills and valleys. The rocks rolled under my shoes and made the bruises hurt.

The sandstone cliffs rose straight up to Curly, so we walked along the bottom till we found a valley the water had cut back into the rock. That's how we got up. I had to drag Essie by the hand.

We were sweating as we went up, and we were dirty from sleeping on the ground. It's hard to stay clean in the woods. Essie had dirt in all the creases of her neck and elbows. She was her true sow-pig self. We panted like crazy when we got to the top of Curly.

We stood in the sun, panting and looking out over the country. It was green, just dark green as far as you could see. To the west, the ground went down from us to Bear Creek, then up again to hills, then down to flat country and up and down forever till the land turned to milky haze and met the sky.

It looked about the same in all directions. Far east of us, some kind of tower stuck up from the woods. We could barely see it. We saw smoke three places in the north and something flashing like a mirror. Nowadays it's not like it was for old-time heroes like Lewis and Clark. They could be alone in the woods. Now the world's crowded, there's hardly anywhere you can't see sign of people.

Essie stared off real keen to the west. I figured she must be looking at the line of sycamores way off there along the North Fork, but she wasn't. She's got good eyes.

All of a sudden she said: "I see an airplane."

Now I could hear it, but I couldn't see it.

"Where?" She pointed, and I saw a blue dot buzzing over green trees and rising higher as it came toward us.

"What are we gonna do, Emmett?"

"Hide!" I said. I didn't even think about it. "Hide!" She ran before I did, right into some bushes, and ducked down between two boulders. I was right behind her. I looked out through bushes and saw the plane was a blue-and-white twin, maybe a new fancy Beechcraft. It banked and came past just level with the top of Curly. The sun shined in through the windshield. I saw everything in a flash.

The pilot looked at the mountain as he flew past, but the other guy in the front seat was slumped down, looking straight ahead. One of the women in the back seat was waving her hands, talking to the other one.

The plane got smaller and smaller, flying away. They flew right over where the Taylorcraft crashed, but it was buried too deep in trees for them to see. Me and Essie crawled out from between the boulders. "They weren't looking for us," I told her. "They were just going somewhere."

"Then why did we hide?" Essie asked.

"I don't know. This is supposed to be our hideout." Essie and me just stood there awhile. Five crows came flying along that cliff below us, kind of rolling in the air and flapping lazy the way they do. Some little bird with a nest in the cliff flew out and started diving at them.

84

He was smaller than my hand, but he hated them nest-robbing crows and went after them like a hero. They just ducked the little bird and ever so easy flew on.

"Let's eat a crow," Essie said.

Here a few days ago she said *Yuck* about a seagull, and now a crow was starting to look good. If you could catch one and roast him, I bet a crow would be delicious. Anyhow, we didn't see anything on that mountain we could catch to eat. Going down, though, we found a different way around the cliffs, a long chute of sandstone with bushes growing at the sides. Halfway to the bottom, Essie perked up.

"I see blackberries," she sang out.

There was a good bush on her side. It was too early for blackberries, but this bush was in a sunny pocket. It had a few purple berries. They tasted sharp as a lemon and sweet as a Hershey both at the same time, but way better than a Hershey. Essie's hands and mouth turned purple before she was through. We even ate some green ones.

We got five minutes of good out of that bush before they were all gone. The blackberries just made me hungrier, but they were one thing we got by trying something different.

We crawled on down the chute and started walking south at the bottom of the cliffs. Where the cliffs cut back to the east, a ledge of rock stuck out farther and farther over our heads. Pretty soon it made a roof that shaded us and then, as we walked farther, an overhang so wide that Essie and me called it a cave.

I looked at the ground, just brown sandstone and brown dirt, and started seeing chips of gray rock scattered. I picked up one about half as long as my thumb. It was flint, and it wasn't all gray. It had streaks of white. Somebody had chipped tiny chunks away to sharpen the edge. It wasn't any lance point, but it could be part of one.

I stuck it in my pocket and said: "This is where Daddy's arrowhead came from."

"The one on his dresser?"

"Uh-huh."

I didn't see my dad's and Emmett Corvin's initials carved on the wall like my dad said, but I knew this was the place where the mastodon hunters lived. It was last Thanksgiving when my dad took me with him to that expert guy who collects Indian stuff. He's the one who said the lance point was seven thousand years old.

The Indians made some beautiful lance points in those days, the guy said, but the particular Indian who made my dad's lance point was a klutz. The blade wasn't quite straight, and that Indian probably dulled the point sticking it in a mastodon. Then he broke off the back corner trying to pull it out. Me, now, I thought that Indian must be a pretty stout klutz, going out every time he got hungry to stab himself an elephant and bring it home for supper.

One place in the mastodon hunters' cave was high as a church. It was dim like a church, too, and the light was the orangy color of the ceiling rocks. Mud-dauber wasps had glued their nests to the ceiling. They buzzed, and we heard the echo of their buzzing.

It wasn't such a bad place where those Indians lived. I could look out from their home and see a lower mountain to the south and then just woods south and west. By now there was smoke coming from a place in the south—far, far away.

I wondered if it was prairie when the mastodon hunters lived here. I wondered if they could look out and see the mastodons when they came to drink in the creek. But I was beginning to figure out how they had the courage to go out and kill an elephant with a sharp rock tied to a stick. You'd just have to be hungry enough. Essie walked out near the edge, where the sun was shining bright. "Look what I found!" she yelled, and the echo said, "I found, I found. . ."

"Shhhhhhh!" I said, and heard it twice again. "Shhh. Shhh."

You had to talk low in that place.

What she found was just a curved white line in the dirt, and not very curved at that. She scratched around the line with a stick till she could grab hold and pull something up. This line was the edge of a white shell the size of my hand, like a clam shell or mussel shell. She kept digging and came up with another, then another. They were chalky white, but you could see they once had a black crust on the outside. Pieces of the black were still there.

While Essie dug, I walked around her and started seeing more of those white lines. They went way down the slope in front of the rock shelter. I saw there was a pile of those shells bigger than a pickup-truck bed and about ten feet deep, all mixed up and buried with dirt.

"There hasn't been water this high in about a million years, Essie. Somebody carried the mussels up here. What do you reckon for?"

"I bet they ate 'em," Essie said.

Maybe that's what the old-time people ate between the mastodons. I picked up two halves of a whell and fitted them backtogether. At one end it made a white wedge, which would be a black wedge if the crust hadn't flaked off.

"That creek down there is full of these things," I told Essie. "I been bruising my feet on 'em."

Her brown eyes got big looking at me, and her blackberry-purple mouth opened in an O shape. That's just what she said, too: "Oh."

17

IT TOOK US maybe an hour to get back to the creek, which is where we started that day. Another half hour and I had a pile of black mussels out on the bank. The mussels were shut so tight I couldn't even get Dad's hooked carpet knife between the halves. They didn't want to get eaten any more than the crawdads did.

I found the coffee can and washed it out real good. That's all the pot we had. I built up the fire and heated water in it. Essie couldn't forget how we used that coffee can the last time.

She kept saying: "Yuck. Yuck."

"Essie, you're way too finicky."

When I dropped a mussel in the boiling water, he opened right up. I cut out a chunk of meat the size of an ear. Fact is, it looked a lot like a prizefighter's cauliflower ear I saw in a picture. I dropped in another mussel, and he opened up. Essie quit saying *Yuck*, but then she couldn't stand the sight of the mussels getting killed. She covered her eyes with both hands. I'm just glad it wasn't puppy dogs.

Pretty soon I had a stack of meat, which I dumped back into the hot water—figured I would make soup of them the way Captain Bligh did after the *Mutiny on the Bounty*. After a while it was bubbling nice and starting to smell good.

I wished I had cabbage palm to put in, the way Captain Bligh did. Captain Bligh was mean, but he was also brave and smart. The guys that mutinied on his ship made him and a bunch of sailors crawl down into a lifeboat in the middle of the Pacific Ocean. It was hard for those sailors, just staying alive. That's what the book said.

Once, they stopped their lifeboat on a desert island, and he told his men to get mussels and oysters and lobsters and even snails to boil for stew. They put in the tops of some palm trees that looked like cabbages. They ate till they were full, and it made them strong. Captain Bligh sailed that lifeboat five thousand miles to civilization. They went through storms and nearly starved a dozen times, and only one of his men got killed in the whole trip. Captain Bligh was a great hero.

But thinking about his stew only made me hungrier. After a while I hooked out a mussel with Dad's carpet knife and gave it a try. It was too tough to chew, so I choked it down whole. After another hour I tried again—still tough. We cooked and cooked that meat, and I found out one thing: You could right away swallow the mussel whole, or you could cook it two hours and swallow it whole—take your pick. But you couldn't dent them ears with your teeth.

They tasted good, though, and it was the first time since we left home that we had all we wanted to eat.

It was also the first time Essie turned whiny on me. She sat back against the tree trunk, panting because her belly was tight. Slowly, slowly, her face turned as sour as the blackberry juice around her mouth.

"Emmett, I'm *tired* of being dirty," she told me. "I don't *like* sleeping on the ground. I don't *like* getting wet in the rain. There isn't even any toilet paper."

"Essie," I told her, "we just need to hide out awhile in the woods."

"I don't *like* hiding out, the way we hid from that plane this morning. What good does it do, hiding out?"

I didn't answer. I just sat quiet, thinking how our social-studies teacher took us once in the school bus to city court in Kansas City. It was clean and nice in the courtroom with pews to sit on like at the Baptist church. But when they opened a door at the back, I saw jail bars behind it. I saw whiskery bums and drunks, filthy dirty, with sores on their arms.

Flying the Taylorcraft down here, I knew what good it was to hide out. Hiding out would keep me from going to that court and being put in with the bums and drunks. Then Essie asked me that question. All of a sudden it came to me that the longer I hid, the longer I would be in jail afterwards. I never told her that.

"*Emmmmmm*-mett!"

"Essie, I don't know. I guess someday we got to go home."

"How will we get there? Will we walk?"

"It's a long way just to the first road," I told her, "and you know what these woods are like."

She pouted her purple mouth at me. "What are we gonna do?"

I didn't answer. The smoke from the fire hurt my eyes, and the bruises hurt my feet.

"*Emmmmmmmmm*-mett!"

"Maybe we'll get rescued," I said.

"Like on Gilligan's Island?"

"I hope quicker than that."

"Them people in the plane today could've rescued us," she said.

"They couldn't either. After they landed here, they'd need rescuing themselves."

90

"If we didn't hide, they could've sent somebody else for us. We could still dig up some white mussel shells and write H-E-L-P on the mountain, like they did on *Gilligan*."

She was right. With all the planes flying past, pretty soon somebody would see it.

"Essie, I don't want just anybody rescuing us."

"Who do you want?"

I didn't say anything. I started wondering what my dad was doing. I wondered was he watching the planes take off, or was he looking for us. I hoped he was looking for us. I just hunkered by the fire, waiting for Essie to jump me again with that *Emmmmm-mett* stuff. This time she didn't. I guess her pinhead brain finally wore out on the subject. She yawned so big I could see blackberry seeds in her teeth.

"That one story you told was all about you," she said. "Tell a story about me when I was little."

Essie said that one story was about me. Did she mean the one about *me* and Mom and Dad in the car, or the one about the brother who treated his baby sister terrible? I never told her that brother was me. Before she could start getting any nosier, I quick started a different story.

"Well, Essie," I said, "do you remember how when you were little, old Willi used to love your rubber pacifier?"

"I like that story," Essie said. "Tell me that one."

I told her how Willi was just a pup then, and every chance he got, he would grab her pacifier and toss it in the air and play with it. He was crazy for that rubber pacifier. Mama had to hide it or keep it high off the floor.

One day Willi sneaked in and raised up on his hind

legs. He raised up like a cobra and stuck his snoot between the slats of Essie's baby bed. He grabbed the pacifier and ran, with everybody in the house chasing him to get it back.

We trapped him in the living room, but he stuck his head in the corner under a chair where he thought nobody could reach. Daddy squeezed his hand in there and grabbed the slobbery, slippery end of the pacifier.

Willi growled and jerked back. He slowly worked his teeth up on the rubber, trying to get a better grip. Then, gulp, it slipped out of Daddy's hand. That pacifier flat disappeared. Willi went gulp about twice more and backed out from under the chair. He stood there with his runny eyes wide open. He was the worriedest-looking hound I ever saw.

Mama called the vet and asked what to do. He said if Willi didn't vomit, everything would be all right. Just keep a sharp watch on the back yard. Two days later, just like the vet said, the pacifier came out Willi's other end.

"And you know, Essie," I told her, "Mama washed that pacifier and washed it, and she like to never got it clean enough for you to use again."

That's when Essie rose up just like Willi did, she rose up like a cobra out of the leaves beside me. "That's a lie, Emmett Ragsdale!" She whacked me on the chest. "I heard that story lots of times before, but I never heard the last part!" She whacked me again. "You made that up!" Whack, whack. I was weak from eating so much, and I was weak from giggling.

"That wasn't *my* pacifier," she said. Whack. "That was *your* pacifier when you were a baby. Wasn't it, Emmett?" Whack. Whack. I was laughing so hard I couldn't even feel the whacking, but then she sat on my chest.

"That was *your* pacifier!" she yelled, and she bounced.

"Don't!" I grunted.

"Say it! Say it was yours!"

"It was yours!" I yelled back at her, but then she really bounced. "Okay, okay," I groaned, "it was mine. That was my pacifier, mine, mine."

She kept bouncing anyway. I looked up and saw something on her neck.

"Hey, quit," I said. "I see something."

She kept grinning and bouncing.

"Quit!" I grabbed her so she couldn't bounce. She was still grinning and panting. I looked close at her neck.

There were white marks about the size of my thumb swollen up above the skin around. The skin looked red and scaly. It wasn't an hour since she ate those mussels. That was the fastest she'd ever started swelling up. She was breaking out with red skin and white marks all over her neck and chest and arms.

18

ESSIE HAD A bad night, then everything got worse in the morning. That day was the worst day.

Her neck and chest swelled up, but her face swelled the most. Seemed like it would stop swelling as long as I watched her. But if I went away a while, like to get her a drink of water, I could see when I got back that it was swollen worse. I stayed with her and kept looking at her, because I didn't want it to swell.

"I don't feel good, Emmett."

"I know it, Essie."

She lay limp on her back in that bed of leaves by the creek. It was shady under the trees but starting to get hot.

"What am I gonna do, Emmett?"

"I don't know."

Her face looked like my mom's bread dough after it rises, only goosepimply and knobby and spotty red. That was bad enough. Then her breathing started getting hard. Sounded like she was sucking air through a sponge wet with water. The asthma is easy to stop if you got the medicine. Daddy stops it quick with a shot. I got scared because we didn't have the medicine.

"Come on, Essie, we got to go up on the mountain."

"I don't feel good."

"We got to get help," I told her. "We got to be where somebody can find us."

I pulled her up and held her and walked her through the woods. Essie panted and gasped, but she tried to walk. We reached the place where the path got steep before she fell down on her knees.

"I feel awful."

She started vomiting. First she vomited the mussels, which looked like they did when she swallowed 'em. They came out whole. The mussels were good for the mastodon hunters and good for me, but they were terrible for Essie. She vomited green water and after that nothing, but she kept on vomiting and making grunty, choky noises.

Always before, I thought it was funny to call Essie a pig. Now she was down on the ground like a pig, making noises like a pig, and it wasn't funny. I couldn't stand to look at her.

I patted her on the back and looked off in the woods. "I'm sorry, Essie. I'm sorry I got you in this mess."

"You couldn't help it."

I could've helped it. I didn't have to fly her to this lonely place. But I was glad she said it.

After the vomiting, she couldn't get up. She rolled over and tried to sit up. Her eyelids drooped like she was sleepy. When she lay back all of a sudden, I thought she was dying.

"Wake up, Essie! Wake up! We got to climb the mountain."

"I don't feel good."

"Come on, get up."

She tried, but she couldn't. I knelt down and pulled her up piggyback on me. She slumped over me with her face beside my face. I could hear that loud breathing. She looked like bread dough, and she lay on me like a heavy blob of bread dough. I thought I could never carry her up there.

I got soaked with sweat and panted like mad, with my shoes sliding back in gravel. A few times I had to hold her with one hand while I grabbed bushes with the other to pull myself up. The wind helped me. It was blowing hard up the side of the mountain. We got to the top of Curly, but I don't know how. That day I did stuff I could never do again.

I put her down on some grass in the shade of a scrub oak. Then I went back to bring her water in the coffee can. I scratched enough old mussel shells out of the rock shelter to write H-E-L-P on a flat ledge of rock. Finally I just sat beside her at the edge of the cliff and looked out to the west toward home.

The sun was shining, the puffy clouds moved fast on the wind, but no airplanes flew past. I was afraid to let Essie sleep. I kept waking her up. I figured if she died now, it would be my fault. I flew down to these woods because I thought I could take care of us. I would be a hero and take care of us.

I was a hero like a German pilot I read about in one of my dad's books. Hans Ulrich Rudel was a great hero, braver than any American pilot. American pilots had to fly maybe ninety or a hundred war missions. Hans Rudel flew twenty-five hundred war missions in his Stuka dive bomber.

A few times he flew with one leg amputated and the other in a cast. He sank a Russian battleship and bombed his enemies and got shot down a dozen times. He was a great hero but never paid attention to what he was a hero for.

He did it for Hitler, that's what my dad told me. Hans Rudel helped Hitler kill millions of people. Maybe he didn't know that, but he should've known it. He fought right to the end and kept the war going longer so that more of his own people got hurt and killed. That's the kind of hero I was. I hurt my own people.

In the early afternoon Essie motioned for me to lean close. She said, "I don't feel good, Emmett."

"I'm sorry, Essie."

We got rescued all right, just in time when we needed it. At least that's what it will seem like when you read this. But to me it wasn't on time. The sun slowly, slowly crawled down the sky in the west, and Essie got sicker. Seemed to me forever that we needed help and it didn't come.

When it's high up, the sun is little, but it gets huge when it goes down. I don't know why. The air around the sun was yellow and thick like orange juice. I felt Essie's hand squeeze my wrist.

"I hear a plane," she said.

When I listened, I heard it, too, over the noise of the wind. For the longest time I couldn't see anything. Then something flashed at me, and I saw the wind shield shining in the sun. The plane was flying far away over the sycamores along the creek. Then it turned and came right at us.

It was a single-engine plane, which rose higher till it was just a black spot on the sun. The spot got bigger. It was a blue Cessna 180 with a white strip down the side. I knew it was Tom Weldon's plane. I started feeling sick in my gut again. I started thinking about that courtroom and going to jail.

I jumped up anyhow and waved, with the wind tearing at me. Hawks were flying along that cliff, five or six big hawks riding the wind that blew up it. After I stood up, they got suspicious and rose higher without even flapping their wings. The plane turned over the creek and came back low between us and the sun. I couldn't see Tom's face at the window, but I could see hands waving. I waved back. Essie even sat up in the leaves and waved.

The plane climbed going away, then turned and climbed some more coming back. Essie grabbed my leg and started crawling up me. I helped her stand up. We stood there on the cliff with the wind gusts blowing up around us. The wind blew nearly straight up from the valley, just holding those hawks still in the air.

Low in the west the air was thick, but high up it was clear as honey. The plane came over fat and slow like it was flying through golden honey. The sun shone on the propeller like on the wings of a bee.

Essie tugged at my arm. "Something's gonna happen," she said.

Of course. Anybody would know that. What I wanted most was for him to drop us Essie's medicine and a box of things to eat, maybe some of Mom's lasagna casserole and about ten pounds of weinies for us to roast. Maybe he could drop a couple of blankets to lay over the itchy leaves. That would be plenty. Then he could turn around and just leave us alone, because I didn't want to go home and go to jail.

"Sure, something's gonna happen," I told Essie. "Sooner or later, something always happens."

19

SOMETHING BLACK FELL out of the plane. It was round at first and fell like a ball of lead.

"See, Essie, I told you."

It fell a ways beneath the plane before I could see it wasn't just a smooth ball. There were lumps on it. Then a white streamer like a flag went up behind it, flapping and shining in the sun and getting longer. The ball fell toward the ground, and the flag reached up toward the sky.

I never thought they would drop the medicine and stuff on a parachute. Parachutes cost money. I didn't want them to do all that. The parachute didn't open just instant. The air bulged one side of the flag, and the other side flapped loose for a second before it all snapped out tight. Then the ball beneath it stretched out long and the lumps split at one end into legs. A man was hanging under the parachute.

I couldn't believe it was a man. I felt sicker and sicker. The man just floated there, swinging back and forth like the clapper in the bell at the Baptist church. At first he hung limp like he was dead. Then he raised his head and reached up to grab the ropes above him.

The hawks riding the wind started sliding back from the edge of the cliff. That parachute looked spooky to them. The plane turned and came back close, like Tom was worried about the man floating down. The parachute was pink on one side from the setting sun and gray on the shadow side, and the sky behind it was dark blue. The man turned slowly around so he looked north and then west at the sun and then south and then east at Essie and me. He was closer now.

"That's Daddy!" Essie said.

I couldn't believe it. I couldn't believe I had caused all this trouble. My dad only whipped me maybe four times in my life, but I figured he would whip me now. I wanted him to whip me, because it would make stealing an airplane seem like all the little things I did before to get whipped. I wondered if Jimmy Doolittle wanted to get whipped when he clunked that guy on the head with his airplane tire. I felt sick and scared and glad to see my dad floating in the air.

The wind blew him toward us, but I figured he wouldn't make it to the top of Curly. He was falling too fast. I could see in his face that he was scared, too, because he thought he might hit the side of our cliff. His face was scared, it really was, but he was also smiling crazy the way he smiles when the planes go up. Daddy was level with us and still going down when I saw him pull the ropes to spill air out and push himself farther from the cliffs. He was aiming for a treeless space at the bottom of the cliffs.

But then tree leaves in the valley turned over and a gust of wind blew up past our faces. The hawks soared up like rockets on the wind. The round top of the parachute below us was stiff in the updraft like the moonwalk deal at the carnival. It looked like you could jump out there and walk on top. That's when the parachute stopped going down and started coming up at us. For a second, my dad was hanging right in front of us. He was tied tighter than any plow horse with rope and harness, but he didn't look hitched anymore. His face was scared and crazy and happy.

"Daddy! Daddy!" I yelled.

He didn't answer. He kept soaring up like the hawks. The wind turned him, and his high-topped shoes went over our heads. I saw the inside of the parachute like the pink inside of a seashell. The gust carried him over us, then there wasn't any updraft. Just beyond us it turned into a downdraft, so Daddy landed hard on the ground near us and fell down. The parachute stuff piled on top of him.

"Daddy!" Essie croaked. I ran over and dragged the silky fabric off him. He sat there panting like he'd run all those miles from home instead of flying in a plane. His hands worked at unsnapping the parachute harness from his chest, but he didn't know what he was doing. He still had that crazy-happy look on his face. Every panting breath he took, he would say: "Oh, my God. Oh, my God."

The knee of his bluejeans was torn. I could see white skin with blood oozing from a scrape. I said: "You got hurt, Daddy."

"Oh, my God" is all he answered. His brown eyes were wide open. I could see blue sky in them and white clouds.

Then the 180 flew past Curly close on one side. Tom Weldon's face looked at us real worried out the window. My dad stood up to show Tom he was all right, but Dad was looking at me.

"How are you? How are you kids? Where's Essie?"

I hated to tell him, because it was my fault. "Essie is real sick, Daddy. She's all swole up."

Then he saw her. She was sitting there looking at him, trying to grin out of her swole-up face.

"Aw, Essie, Essie. . ."

He unsnapped the harness from his shoulders and legs, then walked across the white parachute to her. She held her hands flat to him, like to keep him away. "Don't hug me, Daddy. It'll hurt."

He knelt down and put his hands out on both sides of her shoulders, close but not touching. "Poor old Essie. Emmett, what's she been eating?"

"Last night is the first time we had a bellyful since we been here. We ate mussels from the creek."

"Oh, boy, shellfish. No wonder. I was afraid of something like that." He had a white pillowcase, like a sack with stuff in it, tied around his belt. He started undoing the knot. Essie already knew what was going to happen.

"Daddy, I don't want the medicine. I don't want it." But when he pulled out the hypodermic needle from the sack, she closed her eyes and stuck her fingers in both ears.

"Hold still now. You're gonna get well fast."

She didn't even flinch when he stuck her in the arm. She didn't breathe for a minute. Then the tears squeezed out under her eyelids, about a gallon of tears, and she started breathing. Daddy stood up and came at me. I backed away from him onto the parachute. I thought he would whip me. Then he grabbed me and lifted me off the ground. I'm about as big as he is, but he lifted me, and he yelled in my ear.

"I got my kids! I got my kids back! Ho, boy, I got my kids!"

Then he squeezed me till I couldn't grunt anymore, with his whiskers scraping my ear. He smelled like his own sweat. When I was little, I used to stand in the door of his clothes closet just to sniff that salty smell. While he hugged me, I was still afraid he would whip me but had just forgot. I was glad when he noticed we were standing on the parachute.

"Let's get off. It's one of Tom Weldon's chutes, it's a Pioneer chute worth fifteen hundred dollars."

He pulled me over by Essie. All of a sudden, she was looking halfway bright. I'd seen it happen fast before. It was like Essie was a balloon that Daddy had poked a tiny hole in. The swelling had already gone down a little, and her throat opened a lot. She coughed up some yellow stuff.

"Daddy, you jumped out in a parachute," she said. "You really did. You jumped in a parachute."

My dad shook his head and started smiling crazy again. Just the edge of the sun was still in sight. Daddy's whiskery face was orangy from the color of it, but his eyes were blue again from the sky high up and white from the clouds.

He said: "I let go. I grabbed the wing strut and stood out on that wheel fairing. Then I let go. It wasn't like falling, it was more like flying. I did it. I never thought I would."

My dad did it. I saw him, but I couldn't believe it either.

"What did you see?"

"I saw clear to Mountain Grove. I saw the water tower and the Tindall elevator. The other direction, I saw Norfolk Lake in Arkansas. There was one big boat and four little ones. I was scared, but after the airplane it's so quiet up there. It's quiet."

"My God," he said, and he sat down on a big rock. He shook his head some more and shuddered out a laugh. "When I climbed out of the plane, the wind jerked at me. It was hard to hold on. But it didn't jerk me loose. I let go deliberate, and I was by myself up there. I let go. I never thought I would."

All that time I had been wanting to get rescued, but I didn't want just anybody rescuing us. Right then, standing on the mountain, I found out who I did want.

20

THE 180 CAME flying down toward us again. Daddy jumped up on a boulder and started whirling his arm like a propeller, around and around. The plane banked and came back over us fast. The wings waggled crazy as it roared away west, like Tom was happy about something.

"What did you tell him?" I asked.

"I told him you're both okay. We don't need any help from the Highway Patrol. Now he'll go ahead and drop the stuff."

"The Highway Patrol?" I said. That scared me.

"Watch out, now. Here he comes."

The 180 came over Curly slow, and a big bundle fell out. It bounced once, it bounced high, and came down in some low bushes. The blankets wrapped around it got torn a little. My dad went over and pulled the ropes off and unwrapped it. I saw rubbery black stuff in there, but no lasagna casserole. Daddy whirled his arms like a propeller again, and Tom waggled his wings again. Then the plane steadied and climbed high and flew off to the west. The sun still shone on its propeller, but on the ground we were in shadow.

"What's he doing?" Essie asked. By that time, she could talk easy again.

"He's going home," Daddy answered. "He'll radio the Kansas City tower and tell 'em we're okay. We don't need any more rescuing. Then the tower will call your mom and the Johnson County sheriff's patrol."

"The sheriff's patrol?" I said.

All of a sudden, Daddy's eyes looked real sharp at me. There wasn't any sky in them this time, just brown eyes looking square in the middle of me.

"I ought to whip you," he said.

Only he didn't really say whip. It was a word with country in it, like "whoup." I like to remember the way he said it. He'd have a hard time whipping me if I didn't want him to, but I wanted him to, and he didn't.

"I really ought to whoup you," he said again.

His scratched-up scarry old hand came out at me. The fingers twisted my ear, and the palm boxed my head almost hard enough to hurt. That's all he did. The 180 was just a dot in the west. We couldn't hear it anymore. I heard a whippoorwill in the woods, and the tree frogs were starting. It was getting dark. Daddy said we should sleep in the rock shelter because it was close, but first we had to carry everything down there.

Inside the blankets were our pup tent and five plastic garbage sacks partly full of things and all the rubbery fabric stuff. The rubbery stuff had metal eyelets with a rope tied in them. Essie poked at the rubber with her finger.

"What's this thing?"

I figured it must be soft packing to keep the other things from breaking, but I said: "Daddy brought it along to make up for the one that Willi ate. It's a giant rubber pacifier."

"You're a liar, Emmett. You lie, lie, lie." By then she was feeling lots better.

"Watch your feet," Daddy said. He was wadding up the parachute to carry it.

It was black dark before we got everything down there

and had a fire built. We heated supper in a pot from one of the plastic bags. There wasn't any lasagna casserole, but Mama sent chicken-rice stuff in a big plastic jar. There was thick cheese in it. You didn't have to chew, it just melted under your tongue into delicious flavors that floated up through your nose and filled the whole inside of your head till you could taste it in your ears.

We ate, we really ate. The fire shone up on the rock ceiling of the shelter, and the light reflected back a little. A coyote yipped down in the woods, but it wasn't lonely now. We were cozy beside the fire. I still wanted to know something.

"Daddy, why did you talk about the sheriff's patrol? Is Mr. Enright gonna put me in jail?"

"First, why don't we fold the parachute."

He just didn't want to tell me. We started folding the parachute the way Tom does it on a big table in his hangar. We stretched the cloth and ropes out long, then folded in from the sides. After a while Daddy started talking, but he didn't answer me about the sheriff. Instead, he told what happened after Essie and me took off in the plane.

He said they called the De Soto police and every airport they could think of. They found out we tried to land at Richards-Gebaur Air Force Base. That's where the jet plane nearly got us. But that's the last they found out.

Some guys in the Civil Air Patrol went up to search for us. Tom Weldon did, too. Mom and Dad called everybody we know around Kansas City. Our story got on the TV news, but nobody found a wrecked Taylorcraft. Nobody close had seen us, so they kept calling farther and farther away.

Then Daddy called Alva Cody, the guy who bought

Granddad's old farm. Alva didn't know we were even lost. He doesn't have a TV because the mountains block it off.

"Finally Alva started remembering a blue plane that flew over," Daddy said. "The sun was behind it. He couldn't see good. But he said you turned around and came back over again like you wanted to see him, or wanted him to see you.

"That's when he saw the yellow rope hanging off the tail wheel. Then you flew on up the North Fork. When Alva said that, I knew right where you were. That happened this morning," Daddy said, and looked at his wristwatch. "About nine hours ago."

So my dad ran out to find Tom Weldon in the parachute hangar and told him what he wanted to do.

"I had to beg him. Tom said he never killed a jumper yet, and he didn't want to start by dropping a beginner in the woods. I told him I would pay him big. I said I never was able to do much for my kids. If they were alive, they needed help, and if they were dead, I wanted to be the one who found 'em. I wanted to do that much."

Dad looked at his hands, which were folding the white silky stuff and brushing off dirt and folding again.

"Tom told me he wouldn't do anything this stupid for money. He made me sign three pages of legal stuff holding him blameless for anything that happened."

Essie listened to him with her mouth open. Daddy was mashing the folds down into the backpack, pulling the canvas up around them, when she squawked out: "You talked about if we were dead. Did you think we were killed dead?"

My dad answered low and trembly.

"No, your mama and me didn't. One guy we talked

to at the Highway Patrol thought you were killed. He didn't say it straight out, but we could tell he thought so.

Daddy held the canvas shut with both hands and looked up at us. He didn't have tears in his eyes, but his face twisted up real strange. Just seeing him made my own face hot. I was embarrassed.

He looked down again and pulled the two sides of canvas together over the silky stuff. He pushed the metal loops on one side up through holes in the other side and started threading a steel wire through the loops to hold everything together. He coughed and cleared his throat.

"We knew you were alive. I told your mama, Emmett has stood out there all his life watching them planes land. He knows what a stall is. He's even flown in a plane and held the yoke. He could bring it down safe." Daddy pushed hard on his left hand to thread the wire through a loop where it stuck. He was all hunched over on the parachute. He looked about a hundred years old.

That's the first time I really found out what I had done. Some of this trip I thought we were on a big adventure like Jimmy Doolittle or Lewis and Clark. Not anymore. I didn't feel guilty, I just felt sick, like there was a ball of iron in my gut. That's the sickest I ever was without throwing up. I felt like the German pilot who hurt his own people. That's the worst I felt the whole time, and not just because I hurt my mom and dad.

"You never answered me about Mr. Enright and the sheriff," I told him. "Are they going to arrest me?"

Daddy leaned the parachute against a rock and started brushing dust off the canvas. He didn't even look up.

"As long as he thought you were lost, old Enright

didn't say much. But when your mama called him to say I was going to get you, you might be alive, he got mad on the phone. Don't worry about it, Emmett. He won't do anything if your mama and me can help it."

21

MY DAD WASN'T much different, but he was a little different. Jumping out in a parachute did something to him. After that, he was like a grownup because he knew how to do stuff, but he was like a kid because he wanted to do it. He wanted it. He liked it. From then on, we went pretty fast, everything just awhirl like the current on Bear Creek.

We took the toolbox and some rope down to the Taylorcraft next morning. Daddy wanted to see the plane, maybe take out the compass and whatever else was worth saving. Me and Essie stood below on the dead leaves while he climbed up.

"Hey, this engine ain't hurt," he yelled. "Toss that set of socket wrenches up here."

The wrenches went up, then the bent propeller fell down. Daddy had me tie a rope to a tree trunk and throw the end up to him. He looped it over a heavy branch and tied it to the engine. After a while the engine slid slowly out the front of the plane and hung on the rope. He crawled out of the tree and we both held the rope to let the engine down. Sticking out of the sides were four big cylinders with rusty cooling vanes. That engine was heavy. Together me and Daddy could barely lift it off the ground.

"What do we want with the engine anyhow?" I asked him.

"We'll take it back to Mr. Enright," Daddy said. "Maybe that'll cool him off a little."

I wondered how we would ever carry it all the way home. Daddy pulled out his big Navy knife, the same one he used to save Emmett Corvin's life, and chopped some hickory poles. He made a travois like the ones Chief Joseph and his people used in their last escape from the U.S. Cavalry. Daddy had read that book, too. We used it to drag the engine as far as the creek and then stopped beside the pool where Essie and me had camped.

Daddy said: "Emmett, I'm gonna build a rack to set the engine on. You run back to the rock shelter and bring the boat."

"Boat?" I said.

"Uh-huh. The rubber boat. Go bring it, will you?"

I didn't know what he was talking about, but I didn't want him to know I didn't know. I was halfway up there before it came to me that the black rubbery stuff wasn't just soft packing. It wasn't just a boat, either. When I carried it down and unrolled it by the creek, I found three life preservers in the middle and two paddles that screwed together and a rubber pump that you stomped with one foot to fill things with air. Daddy started hooking up the pump.

"Tom Weldon had to get the plane ready," he told me, "so I drove in to buy the boat at the Army-Navy Surplus in Argentine. It cost $69.95. You're gonna pay that yourself, young sir, out of what you earn sacking groceries for Fleming Brothers."

That really got me. The guys in *Skywolf* or *Blue Thunder* or *Knight Rider*, they maybe crack up a boat or crash an airplane or blow up a car. Then they just go pick up another one for the next TV show. Not my dad.

He's a great guy, but I found out he's cheap when he does hero stuff.

Anyhow, Essie got to stomp the pump and fill the boat up with air. She liked it for a while, but the boat was big. It could hold eight men all crowded up. She kept stomping and stomping and after a while said: "How come Emmett gets all the fun and I have to do the boring stuff?"

It was fun all right, doing what I did. We put the rack in the boat and lifted the boat into the water. Then we pushed and groaned and slid that engine on the poles till it rested on the rack. It was so much fun I sweated myself slick. I scraped the scab off that big gash in my arm so it bled again. My dad squashed one finger, and the nail turned black. But we did it. There was plenty of water in the pool to float the boat and engine and everything. I could see it was too shallow in the first run below. Most of the creek didn't have enough water. After we got the engine loaded, Daddy stood up panting and looked at this one black cloud in the sky southwest of us.

"Now all we need is a rain," he said.

And the cloud answered: *"Boom!A-rooom!Aaa-roooooom!"* It *did*. I swear it did, but the rain didn't start.

Daddy told us that when it finally started, the creek would rise quick and go down quick. We had to get everything loaded in the boat, then sleep on the creek bank and be ready to go.

All three of us carried one load from the cave to the creek. We set up Daddy's pup tent on a grassy rise by the pool. It doesn't have a floor, so we ditched it real good to keep water from running under. Essie was tired. She lay down in the tent while Daddy and me climbed back to the rock shelter for the last load. Daddy took the parachute and slung it over one shoulder. I grabbed the last plastic bag and followed him.

"It's starting to drizzle," he said.

Then he stopped to look at the rock where the wall curved back. I couldn't see what he was looking at. I moved my head a little and saw an A on the rock, which was the last letter of a name, AMOS HOCHSTEDLER, which somebody had scratched in the wall. Behind that name was scratched 1909. I started seeing other letters, no whole names but lots of initials. They were mostly covered with gray-green mossy stuff. On the right side were Emmett Corvin's initials carved big and my dad's initials carved lots smaller. That's where my dad was looking. He stood staring at the names like he was back in Granddad's barn, like he was zapped again by remembering. I still wanted to know the ending of Emmett Corvin's story.

"People don't just disappear," I said. "I bet Emmett Corvin didn't disappear."

My dad didn't answer. He kept looking at the rock.

A blue jay hollered in the woods outside. Otherwise, it was so quiet I heard my feet scrunch in the sand.

I said: "Did you mean Emmett got rich, then he just didn't come around to see you anymore?"

This time Daddy looked at me. "You worry too much about people getting rich. It's hard to be successful, then go back and see everybody you knew before."

"Is that how he disappeared? He just didn't come back?"

Daddy grunted like I was poking him with a stick. "It's no big deal."

"If it's no big deal, how come you won't talk about it."

"Ain't I talking about it?" my dad said.

He never would've talked if I hadn't kept poking him,

but then he did. He stood there and told it. Daddy said Emmett finished his Navy piloting and then had three other pilot jobs in different places and finally went to Kansas City for the best job in the world.

Emmett got to be a pilot for Mercy Flight, which is a hospital ambulance deal where you go out in a helicopter to help people. Once he flew out in country where not even a Jeep could go and brought back a boy hunter who was accidentally shot in the gut. The doctor said the helicopter was all that saved the kid's life. Another time Emmett saved three people, bringing them back quick from a car crash way south of town. Every day they let him do that kind of stuff. Daddy said he was all the time reading stories about Emmett Corvin in the *Kansas City Star* and tried not to be jealous.

"He had the best job in the world," Daddy said. "He had three cars and a big house in the Country Club district. Sometimes, when I was in town, I drove past just to see it."

He didn't hear about Emmett for a while. Then one day Daddy was rolling his dolly with pop cases on it into a restaurant. He saw Emmett sitting at a table with a real rose on it. Roses are cheap, my dad said, you can buy a rosebush for four dollars at K mart and have flowers every summer. But when you see a rose in a little vase on a white tablecloth, then you know it's a real expensive restaurant.

At first Emmett was sitting with another man, and he didn't say anything to Daddy. Both of them were wearing suits, and my dad just had on his coveralls. But when Daddy put the pop in the back room and came out again, the other man was gone. Then Emmett said hello real friendly. My dad stood by his table, and they talked some about Emmett's folks down in White River country. Daddy finally asked what it was like to be a pilot for Mercy Flight. Emmett said he'd quit that job of flying helicopters and now had a better job selling them.

"There's good money in commission sales," Emmett told my dad. "The people buying helicopters, they believe what I say, too, because I was a pilot."

Daddy stood there in the cave and shook his head, like he was trying to get over being zapped. "I asked Emmett why he quit the rescue work with Mercy Flight, and you know what he said?"

"What?"

" 'Because there wasn't any money in it.' "

My dad looked at me like he had said something big. His eyes were just huge, looking at me, like he wanted me to understand. "Didn't Mercy Flight pay Emmett for being a pilot?" I asked. "How did he buy the three cars and the house?"

"Of course they paid him," Daddy said. "They paid him five times more than anybody ever paid me."

"Then why did he quit a great job like that?"

"Because there wasn't any money in it."

Something went click in my head. "Lindbergh wouldn't take money," I told my dad.

"After he flew to Paris, they wanted to pay him so he would brag about their breakfast cereal and stuff, but he wouldn't."

Daddy smiled at me. "I read the same book. 'Course, people loved it when they heard that about Lindbergh. He got famous for not taking money. Just because of it, he was paid big for flying and ended up the richest hero of 'em all."

Daddy had forgot what he was talking about. Then he remembered. "Anyhow, anyhow, when Emmett told me that, I kept on talking like he hadn't said anything. I saw the man sitting there, and all of a sudden I knew it wasn't Emmett Corvin—not the Emmett I grew up with."

"That's when he disappeared?"

"Uh-huh."

My dad stepped up to the rock and pulled his car keys out of his pocket. I don't know why he had his car keys.

He started scratching gray moss out of the initials in the rock so everything stood out clear:

Daddy brushed the dust off Emmett's initials with his hand, then looked at the sky. "She's clearing up. We might have to wait for the rain."

We started down the mountain. Even though the drizzle had stopped, the wet bushes soaked my clothes. The socks went squish-squish in my tennis shoes. I saw my dad's back going through bushes ahead and ran to catch up.

"Daddy?"

"Uh-huh." He turned around.

"Are you sorry you named me after Emmett Corvin?"

My dad was soaked and draggly himself. He reached out and hooked the back of my neck with his clammy wet hand. "No, you're the only Emmett I got left. And you better not disappear. I'm gonna need you on that creek."

22

I FOUND OUT quicker than I wanted to what he meant by needing me. That night we stuffed things in plastic garbage bags so that if it rained they would stay dry, and we loaded the boat. We even covered the Taylorcraft engine with two bags. We blew up the three life vests.

After supper we all squeezed into the pup tent, which smelled like old motor oil and the musty attic of our house. That's where Daddy had kept it for years. Naturally, Essie got the best place in the tent, the grassy spot on the low side. I slept good anyhow right in the middle. I went to sleep, and I slept.

About two minutes later—that's what it seemed like— I slowly came awake with about a million giant snakes hissing in my ears. Right next to me, Essie was slithering around under her blanket like one of the snakes.

"Lie still, dang it," I told her.

"Listen to the rain," Essie said.

The snake hissing was rain. It was like a snake hissing, or a waterfall. It was nearly that loud—a storm with no lightning and no thunder at all, just that tremendous *Shhhhhhhh. . .*

"Now, that's a rain," Daddy said.

It was black in that tent. I raised my head and saw the bumps our feet made under the blankets, sticking up toward the sky at the open end. The tent door was an upside-down V, which was just beginning to brighten up. It was starting to come day. I reached out to the closed end of the tent and touched the canvas low down. Where I touched, I could feel the canvas start dripping. But nothing got on me. I was warm and dry.

"This is a neat tent," I said. "The ditch works great to keep water from running under."

Enough light came in so I could see my dad lying on his side, resting his head in one hand. He said: "That's a lot more rain than Emmett and me got when we were here."

The rain said, *Shhhhhhhhh*. We lay there and listened while the night got brighter.

"Emmett," Daddy said, "what will you be when you grow up?"

"I'm already big as you," I told him.

He didn't say anything. I could see his eyes shining in the dark.

"I don't know," I said. "I might be a pilot, or I might be a cop. I saw a story on TV about a policeman. It wasn't just some dumb program, either. It was a TV news story about a cop who saved a man's life, like you saved Emmett Corvin's life."

"I didn't save Emmett's life," my dad said.

Then this tapping started on my shoulder, this little tap-tap-tap, and Essie said, "When I grow up, I'm gonna be a teacher like Miss Jordan."

"How come you want to be like her?" Daddy asked.

"Because she's nice. Because she hugs us when we do good."

"Maybe you'll be like Sally Ride instead," my dad told her. "Maybe you'll be an astronaut."

Essie's eyes kind of glazed over and she lay back, looking at the tent above us. In a minute she sighed and said: "This is a great tent, keeping us dry in the biggest rain in the world. Ain't this cozy?"

Then Daddy and me lay back, too, and thought how cozy it was. Nobody said anything for a while except the rain, which said, *Shhhhhhhhhh*. All of a sudden Essie thought of something to say.

"Water!" she squalled. "Yaaaaaa! I feel water!"

"What?" I said. "Did you touch the tent and make it leak?"

"Yaaaaaa! There's water coming under!"

Just as I sat up, she started crawling over me to get away from the water.

"It can't be," I told her. "We ditched this tent good." But it was coming under on the low side. She climbed up me like an elephant trying to get away from a mouse, eek, eek.

"You're breaking my ribs, Essie!"

"Put on your shoes," Daddy said. "Then let's fold these blankets and get everything in a plastic bag."

Walking around like squatty ducks in that tent, we did it. We got everything in the bag. I tied it with a twistee and doubled it over and tied it again. By then the whole floor of the tent was water. Daddy duckwaddled through it to the open end and stood up in the rain.

"It's right wet out here," he said.

I stood up with him and felt the rain hit me. It wasn't cold, and it wasn't warm, either. It felt good. I had so much water in my eyes I couldn't see.

Daddy said: "Essie, come on out."

"Not me," she told him. "I'm gonna stay in here where it's dry."

"Honey, it's not dry even now, and it's gonna be lots wetter real soon."

While she was crawling out, I started seeing out what

he meant. I looked around for the rise where we had pitched our tent. The tent was there, but there wasn't any rise. We were standing in water two inches deep, which the rain was whipping hard. That water just got deeper on all sides. There wasn't even any creek. There was just a place where the current roared and sucked and gurgled worse than everyplace else, with the rubber boat dancing on it at the end of the rope. A log floated past the boat and caught on a bush, then rolled over it and went downstream. There wasn't any land that I could see, just cloudy water going away through bushes till trees blocked the view.

"I was looking for high water," Daddy said, "but I wasn't looking to get you kids in a flood."

Essie said: "Daddy, I'm scared." She sounded like she was ready to bawl.

"It's something to be scared of," Daddy told her. "It's dangerous all right, but it's not as dangerous as it looks. Let's get the tent down."

He made us pull up every tent peg and save it. They were cut on a wood lathe, he told us, they were round oak pegs which nowadays might cost $2 apiece. He wouldn't give up a single one. Right in the middle of the danger, he was still being cheap, which made me feel safer, I don't know why.

Daddy made us put on the life jackets. He waded in and pulled the boat back to us. After we bailed the water out, he put Essie in the middle behind the Taylorcraft engine, which was the safest place. Then he sat on the right at the back of the boat and had me sit on the left. He had one foot out on the mud bottom to hold us.

"Emmett, the current will take us pretty fast, but we have to paddle anyway so we can control the boat. When we need to turn right, you'll have to paddle hard on the left side."

I told him okay. He sat there with his wrinkly face turned up a little to that gray morning and water dripping off his nose. Except for the water, I thought his face must look like Jimmy Doolittle's when Jimmy was ready to take off in his B-25 on the way to Tokyo. My dad looked downstream like he figured on finding something nice down there, maybe a cup of hot chocolate with a marshmallow half melted in it and steam rising off the top. He pulled in the foot that was holding us.

"Here we go," he said.

23

TREES STARTED COMING at us. We paddled like mad to aim between the first two, then ducked under low branches and raised our heads to see what came next.

"We have to go left," Daddy said. He paddled hard on the right side of the boat, and I paddled hard on the left till he said: "Lay off, Emmett. You're keeping us from turning left."

I quit, and my dad turned the boat around the next tree. The day was light enough now so I could see hills on both sides, thick with woods. Except for raindrops splashing, the water was smooth for a ways, covered nearly solid with leaves and sticks. It looked like the water and all the floating junk was standing still. We were standing still on it, and the trees were swimming toward us, cutting wakes like the fins of sharks. But the trees weren't moving. We were—and fast.

Everything pinched together at a cliff ahead of us on the right. Daddy stood up and pulled me up beside him on the canvas bottom of the boat. It was like standing with your feet on a bowl of Jell-O.

He pointed and said: "See those ripples ahead?"

The ripples shined like steel in the light from the clouds. They started at the sides and came together like an arrowhead pointing downstream. We both sat down.

"Going into rapids," Daddy told me, "that's where we

always want to hit, the point of the V. That's where the water's deepest."

We hit it. Ahead of us, the creek tilted down steep and the cliff started whizzing past on one side. There were caves in that cliff and trees growing sideways out of it. I wanted to look, but I had to watch ahead.

We went fast a long way down that rapid with water roaring around us into a dark tunnel of trees where the air smelled green and cool. This time the hill of water was so steep we didn't just stand still on it. We slid forward on the water so little waves hit the front of the boat: *Lip, lip, lip, lip, lip.* Essie stood up on her knees to look ahead. Her hair was stringy wet. We went so fast the wind blew it behind her anyway. She held her arms up like the wings of the hawks.

"Wheeeeeeeee. . ." she said.

That's just what she said when we took off in the Taylorcraft, which was also when the trouble started. It wasn't any different this time. We barely slid into this swirly pool at the bottom when behind me I heard sort of a growling like a grizzly bear. Scraping across rocks into the pool behind us was this black log as long as three pickup trucks and big around as a garbage can. It was like a giant arrow with black roots sticking out behind for feathers and a pointy end coming straight at us. Some barbed wire was tangled in the roots. Daddy started paddling.

"We can stay ahead of it," he said.

I hoped that wasn't going to be like staying ahead of a bullet in the gun barrel. It wasn't easy figuring out the creek, which was so big it flowed not only in all the regular places but also in new places. We came roaring down to a Y where the creek split. It looked just the same in both directions.

Daddy grinned real crazy at me. "Which way?" he asked me.

"To the right," I yelled.

I paddled hard on the left side to turn us, and we hadn't gone a half mile when some of the creek's water started flowing away to the left through a willow thicket.

"Aw-oh," Daddy said, "we picked the wrong one." First thing you know, all the rest of the water turned to the left and ran back across a sandbar into the main creek. What we saw—coming at us about a hundred miles an hour—was a willow thicket on the sandbar, which the creek was disappearing into. We crashed into the willow thicket and sort of strained through it. We paddled down crazy crooked ways and bumped against trees and knocked down spiderwebs. Essie hunkered behind the engine and covered her face. Then we got turned backward. Daddy jumped out and held the back of the boat, dragging his feet in mud to turn us straight.

"Whooooo-eeeeeeee!" he hollered.

Daddy hopped back in the boat, and we shot out the bottom of the thicket into the main channel, spitting out leaves, peeling spiderwebs off our faces and flipping the spiders off. Daddy was looking to the left up the creek, where the black log was thundering down toward us. The log had more sense than I did to pick the main channel. We were paddling to get ahead of it when Essie spoke up.

"There's a possum."

We looked to the front. Sure enough, this fat possum had climbed a little willow tree to get away from the flood and then just had to stay. We didn't have time to paddle around him. The boat socked his tree like a 500-pound marshmallow. The Taylorcraft engine leaned forward on its rack, and we all leaned forward, while the willow leaned backward like a catapult cocking itself.

Then the bottom of the willow pushed the boat away, and the top of it flipped the possum. He turned two somersaults in the air and landed on the Taylorcraft engine. Essie was so scared she stretched up tall, she stood on tiptoes. "Yaaaaaaaa! Get him out! Get him out!"

"We can't, Essie. We got to paddle and stay ahead of the log."

"Yaaaaaaaa!"

All the possum saw of Essie was white teeth and scream. He tried to be brave anyhow. He swelled up about the size of a bushel basket with his grizzly white hair sticking straight out. He showed his own horrible mouthful of sharp teeth and hissed like a boa constrictor. That hiss was just a tiny whisper in the middle of Essie's screams.

"Yaaaaaaaa! Yaaaaaaa! Get him out!"

The possum's wide-open eyes looked straight into Essie's kind of startled, like she had shot him. Then he sucked in a big breath and keeled over. He rolled on his side and stuck his feet out. The possum had hairless pink feet with sharp fingernails, about like Essie's hands when she was a baby, only there were four of his feet. Essie got real quiet. She put her own two hands together like she was praying and looked at the possum.

"What's wrong with him? Did I scare him?"

"He's just puttin' on," my dad said. "He'll be all right."

When she turned around, I thought her face would look funny. It didn't. She had tears in her eyes. When they rolled down on her face, you couldn't tell the tears from the rain.

"Is the possum *dying?*"

"No, honey. Haven't you ever heard of 'playing possum'? Well, this is it with a real one. It's just pretend."

She started breathing shuddery like she does. "I didn't mean to *hurt* him."

"He ain't hurt, baby. He's just puttin' on."

"I don't *want* the possum to die."

Daddy held his paddle still and thought about it. "Okay. All right, we'll show you."

We paddled hard for a while and turned three turns, trying to get far enough ahead of the log. Then Daddy lifted the possum by his bare rat tail and set him out on a gravel bar. We pushed off a ways before Daddy reached down to the bottom with his high-topped shoe and stopped the boat. The possum just lay there. The longer we watched, the more shuddery Essie got. We watched a long time.

"Here comes the log," I said. The black tip floated around the corner and banged some driftwood snags and knocked them over. The rest of the log swung around behind. It started sliding down that riffle toward us. "Daddy, we better go," I told him.

"We're okay."

The possum lay there like a lump. I looked at him and to myself said: Dang you, possum, get up! Get up! But he didn't. I started thinking maybe Essie's screams did kill him. I was surprised he wasn't bleeding at the ears. The log was lots closer.

Daddy said: "That possum's all right, honey, but we might have to leave before he wakes up."

"I know," she blubbered. She still didn't believe the possum was all right, but she tried to get over it. She wiped her eyes with the backs of her hands. She shuddered worse and hiccuped and coughed.

The roots on the log gouged the bottom of the riffle. That growling sound came loud through the water under our boat. The creek was narrow there. If the trunk didn't hit us, the roots would and maybe squash us bloody against the bank.

"We got to go," I said.

Daddy kept holding us with his foot. I closed my eyes and felt the raindrops beating on them and to myself said: Please, let the possum be alive. Please, please let him get up. I wondered what Jimmy Doolittle would think about somebody who prayed for a possum.

When I opened my eyes, I saw the front end of the log coming right at us. That's when my dad shoved off and put his foot back in the boat. We paddled fast to get our speed up and stay ahead. It wasn't hard. Daddy knew just when we had to go. I saw Essie look behind and grind her fists into her wet eyes and look again.

"The possum rolled over." She said it ordinary. Then she started bouncing and yelled: "He got up! He got up! He's sneaking off, the possum is, that ratty old possum!"

I just paddled. I wanted lots of room between us and that log before the next thing came up.

24

IT RAINED ABOUT half the morning. My hands got wrinkled. I pulled down the tongue of my tennis shoe to see my foot. It was wrinkled worse and was fish-belly white, like I had spent ten years taking a bath.

But then the rain stopped, the sun came out boiling hot, and we started steaming in the cool air. Looked like the boat was on fire as we paddled through a still place.

I started thinking how every time I hit a lick with the paddle I was coming closer to the Johnson County sheriff. My dad said I wouldn't go to jail if he and Mom could help it. They never had been able to help much against somebody big like Mr. Enright. The big guys get what they want. I figured Mr. Enright wanted me in jail.

"What you looking so glum about?" my dad asked.

"Nothing. You better paddle to keep us straight."

He did, and pretty soon we were back in rapids. We went down Bear Creek way faster than Daddy and Emmett Corvin did. The water was so much deeper we zipped right past the place where my dad saved the other Emmett's life. Daddy didn't recognize it till we went by. Then we shot out onto the North Fork of the White River.

"From here we just got nine miles to go," Daddy said.

"To go where?"

"To the Highway 14 bridge." He rubbed his mouth with one hand and kept his mouth covered. "First we'll stop at a farmhouse and make a phone call so we'll have somebody to meet us."

Essie was standing behind the engine. She turned right around. "Who's gonna meet us?"

"I reckon it'll be your mother."

Daddy pulled his hand down and showed the smile behind it.

"Mama?" Essie said. "*Really Mama?*"

"That's the deal we made, anyway. If Tom Weldon told your mom you were okay, she was supposed to leave the other kids with old lady Summers and drive the station wagon down here. She's supposed to stay at Aunt Mabel's till we can get down the river."

"Mama's gonna meet us!" Essie yelled.

My dad looked at the North Fork, which was muddy and swirly and full of trashy driftwood.

"First let's get there."

After that, the river was way worse than Bear Creek about splitting up into two channels or three or four. It was hard to guess the right way. Once we took a chute of water that left us in a weird flooded bottomland.

These giant sycamore trees rose out of sight, up and up, greener and greener, till you couldn't see the sky on the other side, with tangled vines hanging everywhere and poison ivy and birds going "Awk! Awk!" and snakes swimming through the water. On the far side of the bottomland, the river gathered itself together again and started to move.

It sent us coasting down a channel and pretty quick we found a house high on the bank of the river. It wasn't a farmhouse, it was a fishing cabin, but the people there had a phone. This old woman and man named Yardley lived there. They were glad to see us, because they were worried about the river, which was the highest they ever saw it. The night before, while we were sleeping in the pup tent, that old river tore loose their john-boat and swept it away.

Daddy called Mama at Aunt Mabel's house. Then we sat down a few minutes and drank a Pepsi with Mr. and Mrs. Yardley, because they were lonely.

When we left the Yardleys, the river got crazier. Instead of three or four channels, it was six or ten, with muddy water foaming halfway up the tree trunks. We came swooping out of one channel into another. I heard that grinding-growling noise again and wondered where I had heard it before. My dad looked upstream.

"It caught up with us," he said. "We shouldn't have stayed so long at the Yardleys'."

It was the dang log, big as ever, with the same barbed wire tangled in the roots. It was sliding down the riffle at us, jerking and swinging every time it hit bottom. The tip smacked a green tree with driftwood in the top, and the driftwood floated down before it.

"Paddle, Emmett. We can stay ahead."

Daddy guided us toward the inside of a curve with a little bottomland field on the outside. The river had cut back the outside of the curve, so part of the ground was hanging in the air. All of a sudden, a chunk of the field sagged and slid into the river—pldooooosh!—with green corn still waving when it went under. We were far enough away so all we got was a big wave, which splashed water in the boat.

We were running down this fast chute with a cliff on the right side and trees on the left, when I started hearing something. I heard it, but I didn't want to believe it.

"Daddy, is that a waterfall?"

"On this river there ain't no real waterfalls, but I hear it, too."

We hadn't gained much on the log. Right then the roots scraped the cliff, then got thrown out toward the middle, which made the tip swing across the other way behind us. We came fast around a cedar tree and saw what caused the roaring.

It was a jam of driftwood tangled in willows, which had backed up the whole channel. There were big logs and little ones and sticks and plastic Clorox bottles and pieces of a barn and old tires and a rubber air mattress and a wooden johnboat with the side crushed out. It must've been the Yardleys' boat.

That jam was like a hill of driftwood twice as tall as my dad and filled full of the water rushing through. I started wishing it was a waterfall instead, so we could at least go over the falls. There wasn't any going over this. The whole river roared in there and strained right through. We back-paddled to hold ourselves away. We didn't know what we were doing. Daddy looked back as the log came on fast.

"Paddle!" he yelled. "Go for the trees on the left!"

"We're gonna hit the jam!"

"Paddle!"

We came rushing down on that driftwood hill. You could feel the water suck us to it. I felt like a cockroach in the tub at home, getting sucked down the drain. I ducked under a willow branch that reached out from the left. Daddy didn't duck. He grabbed the branch. It nearly snatched him out. He set his feet in the back of the boat and held on while a wave of water built up behind us.

We swung fast to the left, and the tip of the log went past. The branch swung us into trees—more spiderwebs to get on our faces, more spiders to bat with our hands, and a sourpuss of a fox squirrel to cuss at us while he backed away up a branch.

We nearly got off clean. We would've, except the root end of the log swung around and hammered into the trees after us. Daddy picked Essie up and set her away from it, right in my lap. Then he tried to fend the log off with his paddle. The roots lifted his side of the boat up. I heard scraping and then hissing where the barbed wire poked holes. I set Essie on the tree side of the boat and jumped up. I was scared.

"Let's climb in the trees!" I yelled. "We got to get out before it sinks!"

"Stand still," Daddy said.

When the log swung away, the boat settled back. Air hissed out so fast the canvas on his side was already loose.

"We're gonna sink!" I yelled.

"Emmett, I need you right here."

He grabbed my left hand and pulled it over so two fingers covered the biggest hole. He used one finger of my right hand to cover another one. Then he jockeyed my elbow around to close up the third. The air was just rushing out till I clamped my skin down and stopped most of it.

"Essie, I'm gonna hook up the pump for you to work."

"Okay, Daddy."

I looked up and saw the log angling toward the driftwood jam. The water sucked it fast down the last hundred feet. I heard *Cruuuuuuuch! Splooooosh!* Kind of a wave went through the whole hill of driftwood. The log poked a hole with driftwood sagging in around it. Then the top caved in, and everything let go. It was just a million chunks of driftwood floating away down the river. Daddy saw it and quick tied the boat to a tree to keep us from going down on the current.

"The dang log finally did us a favor," he said. I saw what he meant, because the channel was open now.

Essie stomped on the pump to put air back in the boat. That was sure worth doing. My dad worked at getting the rubber patches ready, which was also worth doing. I started thinking this is the big emergency, this is the big chance to be like Meriwether Lewis on the Long Narrows of the Columbia River. But the best I can do for hero stuff is sit here with my arms turned funny on the boat and take the place of some rubber plugs.

Anyhow, my dad patched the holes, and it was easy after that. We went down the channel with driftwood floating on all sides. It wasn't thirty minutes till we turned right around the corner and saw the start of the Highway 14 bridge. By then, Essie had crawled past the engine to the front of the boat, so she saw everything first. We kept coming around and coming around that corner till I could see the whole bridge. Essie started bouncing in the boat like a flea on old Willi's back.

Guess what I saw next. The very next thing was that dumb old hound, ahead there on the right bank, bouncing around like Essie and wagging his tail and grinning at us. Then I saw Mama standing under trees on a grassy point. She had her feet together and her arms raised up to us, like she'd been waiting there the whole week ready to hug us when we came.

It was great to see her. It was really great, but I started thinking again about the Johnson County sheriff. I wondered what would happen now, and where her arms would take me.

25

I SLEPT MOST of the drive home, and I wasn't the only one. Essie slept stretched out on the back seat, all tangled up with Willi and his fleas. I bet even the fleas were asleep. My dad slept on the right of the front seat, leaning against the window frame with his mouth open.

We were wore out from the boat ride, then loading the Taylorcraft engine and parachute and other stuff in the back of the station wagon. Mom drove, and I slept beside her in the middle of the front seat.

Once I felt Mom's hand slide easy across my forehead and brush the hair out of my eyes. The sun was so bright I'd just as soon she left it alone. But she brushed it real gentle out of my eyes and said: "Did your dad whip you?"

She didn't say "whip" either. She said "whoup" like my dad does. She said: "When he got up there on the mountain, did he whoup you?"

"No. He told me he ought to, but he didn't."

My mom smiled at the road ahead of us. It was a twisty two-lane road through woods and hills.

"I knew he wouldn't. But he should've. He should've whouped you good."

The hair wasn't in my eyes, but she brushed it again anyway. Then she reached behind me and petted Dad on the shoulder and kept one hand there on him while she drove with the other. I looked out through my eyelashes and saw the yellow line of the road rushing back at me. That's when I went to sleep again. Next time I woke up, my dad was still asleep, but now his arm was around me, reaching across so two of his fingers could touch Mama's white shoulder skin. We were on a big freeway road. The sign said: "Springfield, 14 miles." The sun was halfway down the sky ahead of us. It shined on the dashboard dust and on me. I was hot, squeezed up between Mom and Dad, but I didn't mind.

I kept going to sleep and waking up, the way I did when I was little, driving in the car with them, and stars stood still in the sky. I didn't want to be a kid anymore. But right then, just like old times, I wanted everything to stand still like that forever with Mom and Dad and me. Then I opened my eyes, and a sign said: "Grandview, 7 miles." Grandview is pretty close to home. I started feeling sick in my gut again. I started dreading it.

"Does Mr. Enright know when I'm coming home?"

"Uh-huh," Mama said. She kept looking down the road ahead. "He told us we better cooperate. He said he wanted to know, so I called him from Aunt Mabel's house to tell him when we'd get home."

"Is the sheriff gonna put me in jail?"

"They might try it," Mama said. She looked mean at me, like I was the sheriff. "But they're not gonna put you in jail. I'll scratch their dang eyes out."

She said it to make me feel better, but it made me feel worse. By now I didn't mind the idea of jail so much, no matter how dirty or dark it was. I didn't mind the bums and the drunks. What I couldn't stand was the wrong thing I did, and them being polite to me anyways. The sheriff would talk nice and the lawyers would wear suits and talk nice. Mom and Dad and my friends would see how polite they were to me, even if I did deserve what I was getting. I couldn't stand it.

In Grandview, Mama filled the tank with gas. I was glad to stop, because I didn't want to get closer home. The rest of the way, I pushed my feet against the transmission hump, like that would slow us down. Maybe we'd never get to De Soto if I pushed hard enough.

But in no time we were turning off on Kill Creek Road. I wanted her to drive home the back way, which is the long way. Instead, Mama turned on Kill Creek and then on Second Street. The sun was low in the sky. I couldn't believe this was the same day we woke up on the mountain in the middle of a flood, and here we were on the main street of my town.

I saw the aluminum water tower with the Christmas star of lights still up, which they didn't take down when Christmas was over. I saw Snow's Hair Cut Shop, where I have my hair cut when Mama can't do it. I saw Fleming Brothers Super, where I sacked groceries.

For everybody else in town, this was an ordinary day. To me, things looked different, like I was seeing De Soto for the first time or the last time, like I was in a movie or in a dream. Maybe it was going to be a nightmare.

Ahead on the left was an old iron cultivator wheel welded high up to a post under a Budweiser sign. It was Kenny's Silver Wheel Tavern. That's where I saw something that made me sit up quick.

Mr. Enright and a man I didn't know were in the front seat of the Mercedes. The Silver Wheel Tavern is the closest place to the airport where you can buy whisky and beer. Mr. Enright pointed at our car and started yelling. Then David ran out the open door of Kenny's carrying two six-packs of beer, the tall kind of cans.

My dad was awake by then, with a deep crease in his cheek where it had rested on the window frame. He just waved at Mr. Enright as we passed. David jumped in the back seat of the Mercedes. It pulled onto the road behind us and followed.

Old Enright was driving with one hand holding his CB radio mike. He was talking to somebody on the radio. I turned back to the front and saw a tractor stopped ahead of us. The tractor guy was talking to a man in a Chevy hay truck headed the other way. Mom had to stop for them.

Enright pulled the Mercedes up on the right side of our station wagon close to Daddy. I thought, here we go, here we go again, he's gonna bully my dad. Enright and David and the other guy were sitting cool in airconditioning. The window buzzed down, and Enright looked out at us.

Right then it was only about seven o'clock, it was still daylight, but he said: "You're late, Norton. You're way late."

He talked some more real excited and waved his hands, so some of his drink splashed out. It wasn't beer, it was a drink in a highball glass. He called my dad Norton, and my dad called him Mr. Enright. Daddy didn't even look him in the face. I wanted to shrink up and hide.

My dad said: "We brought the engine home to you, Mr. Enright. It wasn't hurt. It's in perfect shape."

"That's real nice," Enright said, "but that doesn't change what's going to happen."

He spilled more of his highball. The other man in the front seat put his hand on the highball glass to push it out of sight below the window. That man didn't have a drink, but David did. He had a beer in the back seat.

He held it low where you couldn't see it easy from outside the car. Enright turned halfway around to the guy beside him and said to my dad: "Norton, this is Larry Brenner. He's a friend of mine and also my attorney. I wanted him along today."

My dad and Mr. Brenner nodded to each other. That's about when the tractor and the hay truck got out of our way. Mama still didn't move our car.

"We'll just follow you on into your place," Enright said. "The sheriff told me he has some deputies close by to meet us. He might even send his field sergeant."

I sat back against the seat like I was dying, but this time my dad didn't just sit back. All the pink color went out of his face. He got white and hard and sat up straight like a stone statue. That's the first time he ever called the man Chester.

"You're not taking this boy to jail, Chester. You're gonna have to take me along. I'm gonna stay right with him."

"Me, too!" Mama said. She was breathing and snorting like Willi does when he chases rabbits. "They better make room for a fat lady in that old jail."

Enright wasn't even looking at them. He was looking at me with green eyes all bloodshot in the whites. The blood in his eyes sort of flashed at me.

"You decided you were gonna run me down, didn't you, sonny. You're lucky I'm not charging you with felony assault. Nobody gets away with making a fool out of Chester Enright!"

He had his drink glass up high again. The lawyer pushed it down and pulled him back from the window. I felt sicker yet, because he was about halfway right. Maybe I did go at him the way I went at Billy Teegarten in our fight. I sat back to hide behind my dad's shoulder, but my dad didn't hide.

He yelled right back: "The throttle was stuck! You ran right down the taxiway ahead of him! Where else could the boy go?"

"I don't know!" Enright yelled. "All I know is, nobody makes a fool out of me!"

"Nobody else needs to, Chester," my dad said. "Let's go home, Dora."

Mama spun the back wheels of the car, the gravel flew out, and she drove us away from them. We went on down Penner Avenue with that Mercedes following. We couldn't any of us talk. We sat there like one frozen statue with three heads, so scared we couldn't stand to look at each other. Essie was lucky. I don't know how she did it, but she slept through all that. Willi woke up and then went right back to sleep.

Pretty soon here on a road from the right came a car which said "Sheriff, Johnson County" on the side. That was the two deputies. Then on a road from the left came another one with the field sergeant. They both turned on their spinning red lights and followed behind the Mercedes.

Next thing, here were two mopeds stopped on a country road at one side with the drivers looking at me. They looked right in and saw me. I figured this must be a dream, because a minute ago I was thinking of Billy Teegarten. Now here he was on a moped with a girl I didn't know on another one. I didn't want him to see me and tell everybody.

"Oh, my gosh. Oh, my gosh."

Daddy petted my leg.

"Just be steady, Emmett, and do the right thing. We'll be okay."

Next after that I heard a roar, and Tom Weldon zoomed overhead, going back toward town. He wasn't in his 180. This time it was his big Cessna Skywagon.

He must've seen the flashing lights and our car, because he banked over a pasture and came back, like he wanted to follow us, too. I spun around and knelt on the seat to watch back there. I saw not just Tom's Cessna but also Billy and that girl. They were following behind the sheriff's cars on their mopeds. If we'd only had a motorcycle cop out in front, we would have been a funeral on the way to the cemetery. Nobody had to tell me whose funeral it was.

I looked down in the back seat. Tangled up there were Willi and Essie with her arm across his tan chest and his black ear flopped over her neck, all wrapped up together and sleeping with their mouths open and Willi's tongue hanging out. Here I am in the worst trouble of my life. They don't care. They're sleeping right through it. The fleas cared more than Willi and Essie did.

That's the way I came home. It was nearly sunset when Mom turned up the lane and turned again into that long driveway. Tom Weldon had taxied his Skywagon off the runway and was just climbing down to walk over to our house.

I knelt on the seat, still looking at what else was coming for me. The Mercedes turned into the driveway behind us, then the first sheriff's car and the second and the first moped and the second. I guess Mr. Enright had finished his highball, because through the windshield and the steering wheel I could see a can of beer in his hand. The lawyer's hand was also on the beer, trying to push it lower in the car so the deputies wouldn't see. Enright jerked back on the beer and held it up anyway. Not even his lawyer was going to tell *him* where to hold a beer can.

I felt our station wagon slow down and stop at the end of the driveway. The Mercedes kept on coming.

The lawyer put his hand back on the beer, pushing it down again. They were kind of wrestling over that beer can, rocking back and forth in the front seat.

I didn't get worried till I saw David in the back seat. He was the only one in their car who was looking out the windshield. All of a sudden his eyes opened wide and scary. He figured out before anybody else what was about to happen.

26

FIRST THING, THE seat back socked into my gut and knocked the wind out of me. Second thing, I flipped over and fell on the floor of the back seat with Essie and Willi on top of me. I had a dog foot in my mouth and then a dog elbow and then only a little dog hair. That didn't help, because even without the dog foot I couldn't catch my breath. All I could do was squeeze out a strangly grunt.

"Uuuuuuhhnnnn . . ."

I did suck in enough to smell Essie's sweat and Willi's doggy armpit and then something worse, gasoline. It was like sniffing the wavy air that comes out of the tank when you're filling it. The car door jerked open right by my head. I saw Daddy upside down and backward.

He started pulling us out of there, first Essie and then Willi and then me. He stood me up twenty feet from the car and waited to see if I would fall down. When I didn't, he let me stand, bent over my gut and sucking for air.

"Uuuuuuuhhhnnnnn . . ." Then the air came. I panted to get enough. It was good and cool but smelled like gas. Mama knelt off to one side, hugging Essie. My dad ran back to the station wagon and started throwing stuff out, the parachute and the pup tent and the rub ber boat. He could've got more through the rear door, but the Mercedes had smashed hard against it, so bad

143

it cracked the gas tank. Gas dribbled out underneath our car.

Here came the deputies, running up the driveway. The one wearing cowboy boots stopped and stood with his hands on his hips, elbows sticking out.

"Look at that!" he said. He ran a little ways farther and stopped again. "Better be careful there!"

David and the lawyer stood under the elm tree looking scared, but old Enright was still in the driver's seat of the Mercedes, yelling out the open window.

"You stopped right in front of me! Why the hell did you have to stop!"

I yelled right back at him. "My mom had to stop! She came to the end of the driveway!"

He looked at me again with the red in his eyes. Then somebody biffed me on the shoulder. It didn't hurt.

"Hey, Ragsdale."

It was Billy Teegarten, saying hello the way he does. That girl was right beside him, looking at me. I couldn't tell where Billy was looking because he had on mirror sunglasses. He was chewing a wooden match between his teeth real cool. Billy's okay, but he gets smart-alecky in front of girls.

"What's happenin', Ragsdale?"

"Boy, I don't know."

That's when Enright threw the Mercedes into reverse and tried to back away. My dad was reaching for more stuff in the station wagon when it started dragging backward. The car bumpers were tangled together. Daddy pulled his head out of our car and ran to the Mercedes.

"Don't! Don't move it, Chester! Cut your motor."

Enright just waved his hand at my dad like he wanted him to disappear. Then he looked back over the seat again and gunned the Mercedes. The bumpers went

144

"Bang!" and broke apart. They must've caused a spark, because fire jumped up beneath our car.

"The engine!" Daddy said.

I still remember how sad that sounded. Then he waded hip deep into fire at the back of the station wagon. He turned the handle and yanked the tailgate door down. It fell off, because the Mercedes had broke the hinges. Then he lifted the top door and started reaching in. The deputies and the field sergeant ran back and forth.

The one with cowboy boots said: "Better be careful there."

I saw Tom Weldon running down across the garden, but he would never make it in time to help. Myself, I couldn't move. I saw Daddy yank the engine. It came half out of the station wagon. He grabbed again and yanked, and I saw him standing there holding the engine by himself. I don't know how he held it. Me and Mama and Daddy all together nearly busted our guts lifting it in there.

All of a sudden the gas tank went "Sssssssssss!" Fire rose up around my dad, rose higher than his head, just white fire with no smoke at all. Mama screamed, and Essie screamed, and then I screamed so loud I couldn't hear anyone else.

My dad dropped the engine and turned half around and walked out of it, with little fires burning in the loose threads of his collar and sleeves and the pockets on his jeans. Tom Weldon got to Daddy first and started slapping the fires out. Mama and me were right behind him, slapping Daddy's back and his butt to stop the burning.

My dad said: "Death by fire would be easier than all this whouping."

"Norton," Mama said, "oh, Norton. . ."

"I'm okay." Daddy smelled like gasoline and burnt

hair, but he was starting to smile. "Whoooooeeeee! Reckon I won't need a haircut for a while, Dora. You won't need to trim my eyebrows, either."

His eyelashes were burned curly. His ears were burned pink, but his thick jeans and long-sleeved shirt helped him. He looked back at the fire and stretched his arms out, shooing us away like we were a flock of guineas.

"Watch out. That thing's gonna go."

Old Enright saw us moving away and he pulled the Mercedes farther away. Then the gas tank went.

"Whoooooomp!"

The doors on the station wagon blew open. The windshield blew out, and one chunk of it spun through the air and broke glass in our kitchen window. A ball of fire rose up higher than the elm tree. The oil in the Taylorcraft engine was burning hot. It sent a puff of smoke up with the fire. David and the lawyer ran like the devil to get far enough away. The deputy held up his Smokey Bear hat to ward off the heat. There wasn't anybody fighting to get closer, but he said: "All right, folks, let's keep back from the fire. Everything's under control."

I heard the other deputy call on his car radio for the Johnson County Fire District Number 3 Volunteers. Then we just stood and watched our car burning hot, with things hissing and popping and shooting up like little rockets and windows breaking and the fenders melting at the back.

Mama stood with Essie's head pulled in to her chest and leaned against Daddy on the other side and rocked both of them back and forth. "Oh, Norton, our car, our car . . ."

My dad didn't look downhearted. After you lose a Taylorcraft engine and your eyebrows, how much is a car?

27

IT SEEMED LIKE more than a car to me. Before that, I already was in trouble. Now it was worse. But that's when Mr. Enright started getting into trouble, too.

We all saw the field sergeant catch the lawyer walking away from the Mercedes with two open beer cans and the highball glass under his shirt. The front of his shirt was wet with beer leaking out. The lawyer looked at the sergeant.

"I was only picking up the litter here in the yard," he said.

The sergeant went sniffing into the Mercedes and found the rest of the two six-packs, which was the same brand of tall-size cans. He held 'em up to the lawyer, who was standing right in front of me with Mr. Enright.

"Litter, huh?" the sergeant said.

My dad tried not to smile when he saw it. He looked at the ground and raised one hand to rub the back of his neck, the way he does when something strikes him funny. The lawyer looked at the hand on Daddy's neck and grunted like somebody hit him. Sort of sidewise to David, the lawyer whispered:

"He's gonna sue. He's gonna claim whiplash."

Whiplash is what happens to your neck when somebody hits the back of your car, that's what I found out later. Usually that somebody gets sued for lots of money, because it's always his fault when he hits the back of your car.

Billy Teegarten stood there in his Jordache jeans with his girlfriend beside him, grinning under his sunglasses. He thought all this stuff was funny.

Then the cowboy-boot deputy walked up behind Billy and put both hands on his shoulders. "Is this the boy we're supposed to arrest?"

Billy stopped grinning and the girl moved back from him.

"Nossir," Enright said, and he pointed at me. "That's the one. Arrest him."

I felt like I would shrivel up, I would die, getting arrested with Billy Teegarten watching.

The lawyer said: "Let's wait a minute here. Let's just think about this." So everybody stood there while the lawyer scratched the side of his nose with one finger. Then he looked at Daddy and said: "You know, we're real lucky nobody was hurt here."

"What makes you think nobody was hurt?" my dad said. "It *feels* like I was hurt. All this talk about putting my son in jail—I'm feeling *bad* hurt."

Afterwards my dad told me he was a rat for saying it, he shouldn't ever've said it, because he wasn't hurt. But I'm glad he said it.

Right then, Enright pointed at me again.

"Arrest him!" he yelled. "Why don't you arrest that kid!"

"No, no, no, no, no," the lawyer said.

He grabbed Enright by the shoulder and turned him around and walked him away from us, hissing at him and talking to him.

Enright broke loose to turn around and yelled: "But why the hell did they . . ."

The lawyer put a hand over his mouth to choke him

off. Then he grabbed him and turned him and walked away again, still talking. To do law work for Mr. Enright, you have to be a good wrestler.

Right about then I heard something go *Rrrrrr!Rrrrrr! Rrrrrrrrrrr* . . . This time it wasn't an airplane, it was Billy Teegarten's moped. He went down the driveway and zapped out of the lane before his girl could even get hers started.

David went over to huddle under the elm tree with Enright and the lawyer. The lawyer and David took sides against Enright. They bawled him out, but quiet, so we couldn't hear. The more they talked, the sadder Enright looked. Tom Weldon came over to stand with us. I liked having him there. Pretty soon the field sergeant got tired of waiting.

"What about it?" he asked them. "You got a complaint against this kid or not?"

David and the lawyer pushed Mr. Enright out of their huddle. He came out with his hands spread open in front of him.

"Let the kid go," Mr. Enright said. "Forgive and forget, that's what I say."

"We're not gonna forget the station wagon," my dad told him.

"It's all covered by insurance," the lawyer said. Now he was smiling big, and so was David. "We'll get you a better car," the lawyer told my dad. "We're just glad nobody was hurt."

They blabbed on awhile about insurance, which wasn't interesting to me. I felt good anyway, and I didn't know why. I started remembering something, like when you're in a bad mood you remember you got a candy bar hidden that you had forgot about.

I wandered back behind the lilac bush. That's when I remembered it: Let the kid go. I sat on the ground and lay back and spread my arms out across the cool grass. The sky was red in the west and was still purple straight above, but four stars shined through it. The crickets had already started. It was getting dark.

"Let the kid go," I said. "Let him go."

I felt the corners of my mouth smile. I breathed the cool air and smiled, because I would never have to go to that courtroom. I wouldn't have to go to jail. I breathed the air and watched the stars stand still in the sky, till all of a sudden Essie was staring straight down at me.

"Get up, Emmett. How come you're lying in the damp?"

" 'Cause I want to. 'Cause it's the place I am in the world."

"Get up."

"Nuts to you. I like it here."

"All right, I'll lie down beside you."

"If you lie down here, I'll get up."

"Well," she said, "I'm durn sure going to lie down."

So I just got up to keep her from lying down beside me. I don't know how she does that. Essie always wins. Anyhow, on the other side of the lilac bush they got tired of talking about insurance, at least the field sergeant did. He started talking like he was thinking to himself.

"So we don't arrest the boy, but we still got this accident. We got careless driving. We got liquor containers open in the car. We got driving while intoxicated."

By the time I got around there, nobody had answered him. Mr. Enright was standing there with tears in his eyes. That's the first time in my life I ever felt sorry for him.

My dad said: "He might've been drinking, but he wasn't drunk."

The field sergeant's eyebrows raised up about a mile. "You're the injured party. Don't you want him arrested?"

My dad was touching the rim of his ear where it was burned pink. He said: "I don't think so—not any more than I wanted my son arrested."

"We could use you as a witness," the field sergeant said. "We sure don't want you as a witness for the other side. Don't you want him prosecuted?"

"I don't believe I do," Daddy answered. "He's my neighbor."

The field sergeant made a noise like a tire going down. At the end he popped his hands together and said: "Wild-goose chase. Now everybody loves each other. Why don't they start loving each other before they call the sheriff? Boys, let's get out of here."

The sheriff guys left, and the bunch in the Mercedes started to. The lawyer walked Enright to the car and started easing him down in the back seat. Somebody else was going to drive this time.

He was about half down, with the lawyer's hand on top of his head, when he popped up again and stood looking at my dad. He said: "Norton, I may get sued out of all this . . ."

"No, no, no. The lawyer pushed him down in the car.

The head pushed slowly up again between the lawyer's hands. "Because I *was* drunk, Norton. I *am* drunk . . ."

"No, no, no." The head got mashed down. David ran around the car to help the lawyer. They weren't big enough to hold Mr. Enright down. He lifted David off the ground. They were climbing on him like King Kong on the Empire State Building. With them hanging all over him, he still looked at my dad and talked.

"If you sue me for injuries, Norton, I'll fight you like

hell in court. But I *appreciate* what you told the deputies."

David bumped the back of his knees and folded him into the car. Then the lawyer drove the Mercedes out of the driveway. It was damaged in the accident, it made funny noises, but it moved.

Then everything got quiet for a minute, it was just super quiet after all that ruckus. The fire had burned down to a red glow. Mama said goodbye to Tom and went in the house to call Mrs. Summers and ask her to bring the other kids home. We didn't have a car to go get them.

That's when the Johnson County Fire District Number 3 Volunteers came roaring up the driveway in their truck and skidded to a stop. Most of the Volunteers were wearing baseball uniforms. When they saw how little was left of the car, they didn't even hop down from the truck. They just looked kind of uneasy at the burned car with the Taylorcraft engine lying on the scorched driveway behind it.

"It wasn't the game that slowed us up," the one in the driver's seat said. "We got to the firehouse quick. Trouble was, it took a while to get the truck started."

"Wouldn't have made any difference," my dad told him. "It was as good as over before the deputies even called you."

That perked up the Volunteers. They started kidding each other about how speedy they were. They all waved as they went out the drive. My dad waved back, and so did Tom Weldon, who was still hanging around. Tom pulled out his old corncob pipe and stood in the driveway sucking on it. He doesn't smoke anymore. He sucks the pipe so he won't want to. He bit the pipe stem between his teeth and talked around it.

"Norton, for a first try, that was one devil of a jump you made on the mountain."

Daddy smiled down at the grass. "All I did was let go."

He looked embarrassed and walked away, over to the Taylorcraft engine. Tom followed him, and so did I. I could still feel heat from the car. The engine was burned black, with the oil pan melted and two cylinders cracked.

"She's a goner," Tom said.

"Looks like it."

Tom walked back and forth beside the engine, scratching his head like he was embarrassed, too. He said: "I liked the way you went after this engine. I really did. You had the guts to try and the good sense to back away when it was time."

My dad shook his head.

"I backed away all right, barely in time. But I was dumb to try it."

Tom never hung around our house before. I wondered why he kept staying. He took the pipe from between his teeth and looked real keen at my dad.

"I'm ashamed to make an offer like this," Tom said. "You'd have to keep your day job, but I'll hire you nights and weekends to work on the planes and help me handle jumpers. All I can afford to pay right now is five dollars an hour."

My dad just stood quiet for a minute like somebody hit him on the head.

"All right," Tom said, "I'll throw in flying lessons and get you a license so after a while you can take up some of the jumpers."

He kicked at gravel in the driveway, acting real nervous. He looked at my dad like he wanted an answer.

The best that Daddy could cough up was: "I get four

dollars an hour on my night job. You're talking about paying me a dollar more?"

"It isn't much to offer, Norton. I know that. I don't have the business yet to *need* you that bad. I just *want* you."

Daddy was standing there like some stupid statue, but I wasn't. I was jumping up and down beside him. I biffed him in the shoulder the way Billy Teegarten biffed me, and I yelled: "Take it! Tell him you'll take it!"

"I'll take it," Daddy said.

28

SO MY DAD didn't get rich like Lindbergh. A dollar an hour is all he got out of being a hero. The job with Tom isn't much yet. It's just a might-be, could-be, hope-it-will-be. He likes it, anyway.

Mr. Enright's insurance bought us a better station wagon than we had before, two years newer, with a neat stereo system. And he quit drinking, Mr. Enright did, after the field sergeant scared him so bad about driving while intoxicated. The most you'll see Mr. Enright with now is a can of Nehi orange.

I did a lot of dumb stuff, see, and still things came out pretty good. That isn't fair, I know it isn't. That's just the way it happened.

Daddy keeps on walking down by the fence to watch the planes go up. Now I walk right with him. Anything he does, I'm gonna do more of.

Here last week an old Beechcraft Staggerwing flew into our field on its way to the air show in Oshkosh, Wisconsin. Daddy helped tie it down, then the pilot went to spend the night with his brother in De Soto. I woke up the next morning just when the blue jays started hollering. Daddy was shaking my shoulder.

"Come on. The Beechcraft's gonna take off."

I went out in my pajamas, barefoot in the dew, because there weren't any women to see me anyhow. The sun wasn't up yet when we got down to the fence. There

155

was just a red place in the east. There were some puffy gray clouds low down and puffy pink ones higher and way, way high some clouds shaped like fishbones. The fishbone clouds were pearly like the top of Mama's music box.

Something said: "Pow! Pow!" Then I heard a whir and the loudest rumble I ever heard from an engine on our field.

"That's four hundred fifty horsepower," my dad told me.

Smoke fogged up around the something parked this side of the hangars. I couldn't see. Then the prop blew the oil smoke away. It was only a single-engine biplane. But it was big, and it wasn't all choked up with struts and wires like pictures I saw of Spads or Sopwith Camels. The Staggerwing was sleek. It had a red engine cowling and a red lightning streak down the side. I figured the rest must be white, but it looked pale gray because there wasn't any sun.

"They built that one in 1936," Daddy said. "It's nothing but sprucewood and glue and fabric, but it can fly two-ten. That's faster than some fighter planes of them days."

It just sat there while the engine warmed. I stood by the fence and felt the dew chilly on my feet. Even without the sun, the wet grass on the runway shined in light from the sky. A meadowlark walked around out there like this was just any old meadow. He was about to find out.

The Beechcraft engine revved, and the plane swung around, then taxied slowly out onto the runway. By the time it stopped, the pilot already had used a third of his takeoff space.

"He better go back," I said. "He won't get that big thing off."

"You watch."

The engine buzzed up again with the plane sitting still. Then the pilot let go his brakes. The Staggerwing shot out like an arrow from a bow. It zapped down the runway with the bottom wing pushed out ahead of the top one, like it wanted to be first in the air. The two front wheels and the tail wheel blotted up the dew and left three black tracks in the shine on the runway.

The tail rose, and it was only two tracks. The prop whizzed up a fog of dew in a blur around the plane. It looked like a gray ghost plane or a spirit plane from old times. That's when the meadowlark hollered and flushed and flew right at us, so I saw the black band on his neck. He didn't want done to him what the Taylorcraft did to that dumb guinea.

Way before the Staggerwing came even with us, the black tracks ended. The plane flew right off the ground. Then the wheels folded to the fuselage like someone folding his hands in over his heart. I saw a dog in the co-pilot's seat. I did. There was a real dog looking straight ahead out the windshield. The pilot raised his hand to my dad as he passed.

When the Staggerwing banked to turn east, I saw the wings were curved around the tips and trailing edges like a Spitfire's wings. The plane flew into one of the gray clouds. I couldn't see for a second. It came out and rose up high enough to reach the sunlight. All of a sudden the gray was gone. The Staggerwing was bright red and white with sun shining in the propeller.

"Golly," my dad said, "oh, gaw-*leeee*. . ."

It rose higher than the pink clouds and kept on floating up against the blue, so far away after a while all you could see was that shine in the propeller. It could never get that high, it never could, but it was climbing for the pearl like it was flying into heaven.